ABOUT TH...

Colm Herron's first writin...
seven when he sold his v...
Two years later he was telling cliffhangers to the wasters in the local gambling hall. Colm's abiding memory is that these guys seemed to enjoy this weekly break from misspending their lives.

When he was fifteen he had a play on BBC and later brought his short stories to Brian Friel, an emerging playwright. Friel said "Great. This stuff's better than what I wrote at your age." But Colm was unimpressed and thought "Friel's going nowhere. I don't know why I came to him at all."

So Colm gave up writing, deciding to live instead. Meanwhile Friel took off and, while his plays were showing worldwide for the next thirty years, stories were kicking and turning in Colm's head. But they still weren't ready to come out. Till twelve years ago, that is, when he said to himself "OK, I've lived. Maybe it's time to do the other thing."

And so began his second writing career...

ACCLAIM FOR COLM HERRON'S PREVIOUS NOVELS

For I Have Sinned

> "Perhaps the greatest tribute I can pay to this quirky, funny and deeply affecting novel is to declare that the moment I finished reading it, I immediately turned back to the first page to begin again. And it's even better second time round."
>
> —Ferdia Mac Anna, *Sunday Independent*

Further Adventures of James Joyce

> "A totally comic novel .... *Further Adventures of James Joyce* could just as easily be entitled *The Further Writings of Flann O'Brien*."
>
> —Morris Beja, *James Joyce Quarterly*, Tulsa, Oklahoma

The Fabricator

> "Fascinating, funny, sad and delightful. From its opening lines right through to its final pages *The Fabricator* is not like anything you have read before."
>
> —Kellie Chambers, *Ulster Tatler*

COLM HERRON

THE WAKE
(AND WHAT JEREMIAH DID NEXT)

NUASCÉALTA

The Wake (And What Jeremiah Did Next)© Colm Herron, 2014.
Visit Colm's website: colmherron.com
Contact Colm on Twitter: @colmherron

All rights reserved.
No part of this book may be reproduced in any form or by any means including electronic or mechanical photography, filming, recording or by any information storage and retrieval or video systems without prior permission from the publishers, Nuascéalta Teoranta.

www.nuascealta.com • info@nuascealta.com
Cover Illustration and Design: © Karen Dietrich, 2014.

Typesetting: Nuascéalta Teoranta.

ISBN-13: 978-1495299735
ISBN-10: 1495299732

A Note from the Publisher

Any seeming grammatical and spelling irregularities in the text relate to the author's intention to reproduce the cadences of Derry speech.

OTHER NOVELS BY COLM HERRON

For I Have Sinned
Further Adventures of James Joyce
The Fabricator

For Nuala

THE WAKE
(AND WHAT JEREMIAH DID NEXT)

I really didn't want to be bothering you about this but Maud Harrigan died yesterday, dropped dead at our kitchen table. No loss if you ask me. But wait till you hear. We're waking her, yeah you got that right, we're waking her. She near enough lived here and she died here and we're not going to get rid of her till she's carried out that bloody door. And in the meantime I have to listen to Mammy's crap.

"Poor Maud, she'd nobody. She was wile lonely since Bobby died. Always looking to do you a good turn so she was." Bobby was glad to get out of it. He was the only corpse I ever saw with a smile on its face. Everybody at the wake remarked on it, one or two that I heard gave the credit to Charlie Bradley and Denis McLaughlin of Bradley & McLaughlin but most of the women at the wake decided it could only mean he was in heaven. I thought he looked more like he'd got out of hell.

Maud was waked in our house for one reason and one reason only. Mammy insisted. I wanted her to be brought to the cathedral to lie overnight as soon as she could be boxed and then on to the cemetery after mass in the morning but Mammy wasn't having it. Fucking hypocrite. The face she showed to the world would have made you sick. She was posing as the selfless neighbour that wanted to give Maud a good send-off and she was landing me with all the arrangements. Typical. And of course she was showing up Majella Doherty, Maud's neighbour on the other side that hadn't spoken to her for years over Maud puncturing a ball that Majella's weans had accidentally kicked into her back yard.

But here's the thing. People that came to the wake were going on as if I'd been bereaved, shaking hands with me and some of them kissing me and telling me they were sorry for my trouble. I was actually going along with it sometimes, mainly because I wasn't able to hit the right mood between that and the distaste I felt for the whole thing. You have to understand, a whole lot of the women in this town are like professional mourners, they come into wakehouses with expressions on them like Veronica wiping the face of Jesus on the way to

Calvary and you have to go along with it or people will only be talking about you. This meant that most of the time I'd an expression of either resignation or desolation depending on who I was talking to.

And then the stressful conversations I had with the two undertakers—these guys put their faces right up to yours when they're talking to you as if what they're saying is really confidential when they might be only asking you where the toilet is or telling you what time the hearse will be taking Maud to the cathedral or exactly where the grave is located, the last bit being vital information of course because I as the chief mourner would be walking right behind the hearse all the way to the cemetery and God knows I might veer off and end up in the River Foyle like one of those horses in the Grand National that didn't turn left at the Canal Turn and had to be pulled out of the Leeds and Liverpool canal.

There was this big hallion of a girl too from over the terrace Majella McAllister that caught me completely unawares and gave me a French kiss at the door when she was leaving and left me standing there with my mouth full of slabber just as the Miss Quinns were arriving. I did manage to get rid of some of it by leaving four small deposits on the two old ones' cheeks, *ucching* most of the rest of it over the wall of Maud's garden as I followed them in. Majella's had a notion of me for years and she used to give me the glad eye in the street till I stopped even looking at her. She was crafty the way she did it though. She was saying cheerio and how good I was to be waking Maud and I thought she was away till she turned quickly as if she was suddenly overcome with emotion which could well have been the case now that I think of it and gave me this warm wet kiss on the cheek and then her big sticky lips sort of slid down sideways to my mouth and that's when the tongue came out.

    I got a day and a half off for this but to tell you the truth I'd far rather have been in school even though I've a Primary Six that would put years on you. Father Swindells arrived about half ten just when the wake was getting into its stride and reminded me first thing that I had to be back by the beginning of lunchtime the day of the funeral seeing I was on playground duty all week.

"You haven't been well lately Jeremiah?" he said, still holding my hand after he finished shaking it. By rights he shouldn't have been shaking my hand at all because he knows full well I've as much relationship to Maud as I have to Ian Paisley. I find him creepy, Swindells that is, face shiny and smooth like a choirboy's and those piercing eyes and curved beak of a nose like an eagle. What's the word? Egalitarian? No, hardly that. Aquiline I think. Yes, aquiline. And there was something yucky about him that was patronising and ingratiating at the same time slowslidingly mingling the sweat of his hand with mine.

"How do you mean Father?"

"You were off a few days, weren't you, this past fortnight? No notice to speak of either. You're not having late nights are you? Not burning the candle the two ways as they say?"

I shook my head. We were still holding hands, perspirations slippily melding. Looking down at him I felt both wary and fearful, wary of what he might find out, fearful of what he could do. He doesn't come up to my shoulder and he makes me feel small.

"Not at all Father. I've been trying to shake

off this flu but it just won't go away. I'm sure you've been through the same sort of thing yourself."

"Yes," he said smiling joylessly, "but I haven't been out on street demonstrations challenging the law and being chastised for it. How are you anyway? It's a wonder they didn't arrest you. That wouldn't have looked good you know."

His shoulders then began to shake with put on mirth. "Have you ever heard the one?" he said, spluttering into his free hand. "I suppose I shouldn't be telling it to you at a wake of all places but what would you say now is the difference between a magician's wand and a policeman's baton?"

I waited in disbelief and then saw from his expression that I was expected to ask for the answer.

"I don't know Father," I lied. "What's the difference?"

"Well you see, the magician's wand is for cunning stunts." He stared at me to see when the penny would drop. I smiled slowly, then nodded approval, indicating that it had. His shoulders shook again, pleased. If I'd told him what I thought in return for the penny they wouldn't have been so pleased I don't think. At this point he removed his hand and left me abruptly, realising I suppose that he was neglecting his duties. As I was mine. Three people were waiting to offer their sympathies. Mammy was nowhere to be seen, having gone upstairs to lie down, possibly permanently. I wiped my right hand on the shoulder of my pullover and went to meet them. I heard word behind me then that prayers were about to be said so I made my apologies and went to the kitchen where Maud was laid out.

Father Swindells was looking solemnly into the coffin, lips moving noiselessly, and after a short time he waved his hand over the corpse in what looked like a gesture of dismissal, begone from me, then moved away and stood with his back against the kitchen door, proceeding to intone a decade of the rosary, flicking his long mother-of-pearl beads extravagantly as he went from one Hail Mary to the next. The mourners responded respectfully, some sitting, some kneeling. When the decade was finished the priest moved forward expectantly, looking for someone to offer him a seat. There were no men occupying any of the chairs so Majella McCorkell, one of the youngest present, got up and said: "Here's a sit for you Father. I'm going now anyway." She bowed her head to him as she passed and he touched her shoulder familiarly.

"That's big of you Majella," he said smiling broadly. "And while I'm on the subject, no word of you starting that diet is there?"

Majella reddened and answered: "No word yet Father."

There were one or two stifled giggles as she went out. The priest sat down, shifting his backside on the chair until it was settled comfortably. He looked around him benignly and his gaze settled on Mairéad McCaughey to his left.

"Hello Mairéad," he said. "And how are you and all the bairns?"

"We're grand Father. We're all grand."

"And Charlie. How's Charlie getting on? Still helping out with the Saint Vincent de Paul?"

"He is Father."

"Isn't he the great one," said the priest. Then duty done with Mairéad the eagle's head rotated ninety or so degrees due west and the black-button eyes found Susan Helferty.

"Ah, Susan," he said. "I see you're with child. How many will that be now?"

"Nine, God willing Father."

He smiled, gratified. "The more the merrier. Aren't you great now Susan. And Bobby's working away. Two jobs still hasn't he?"

"No Father. He was paid off last year from the building and Jimmy Heffron told him he doesn't need him in the pub anymore."

"Oh dear." The priest's indifferent eyes blinked and stared ahead. "Well I'm sure you'll be all right. God will provide, my dear, God will provide."

He was a little taken aback when Susan began to sniffle but sharp enough to lay a comforting hand on her arm. "Now now Susan, don't you be worrying now. You'll see."

But the floodgates were well and truly open. She took a large grey handkerchief from her overcoat pocket and proceeded to weep buckets into it. Father Swindells seemed at a loss as to how to stem the flow but Miriam McBride rode to the rescue.

"Maud went sudden, didn't she Father?" she said.

He looked across at her and smiled, composure restored. "The ways of God are not our ways," he said softly. The blubbering went on unabated to the side of him but the priest was on familiar ground now and raring to go. "Sure none of us knows," he said, fixing his full attention on Miriam, "not one of us knows the day nor the hour. When I hear about a sudden death I always think of that parable Our Lord told about the wedding. You know the one I'm sure."

Miriam nodded knowingly, not knowing the one I'm sure but hoping he'd think she knew. Miriam is what we call in these parts a good-living girl. This doesn't mean she grows her own vegetables or even that she lives it up. No, it means that she never lies out of the chapel, never has a bad word to say about anybody and would never let a man near her.

She was still nodding like a toy dog in the back window of a fast-moving car when Father Swindells went on to talk about the parable of the ten virgins though he didn't say virgins of course. Bridesmaids was the word he used or was it girls? I can't exactly remember. Whatever it was it wasn't virgins because he knew that that particular word was one which should only be used in mixed company when it referred to the mother of Jesus. Otherwise, taboo.

"The bridegroom was late coming if you remember and the five foolish bridesmaids hadn't taken the precaution of having enough extra oil for their lamps. Of course the other five bridesmaids, the wise ones, had plenty to spare but wouldn't part with it when the foolish ones found their lamps were dry."

Disobliging bitches I was thinking when the door swung open and Willie Henry McGillycuddy stood swaying and surveying all before him. He quickly spotted me and hastened forward to shake my hand, face wreathed in sympathy.

"I'm sorry for your trouble Master," he said. It's a strange country we live in when people call it having trouble when someone dies. Granny Coffey used to say a person was in trouble if somebody belonging to them died. Funny word trouble. Hold on, I'll be with you in a minute, I'm having trouble with this shoelace here. Excuse me but could I trouble you for a light? I hear your man Doherty got that wee one Majella what-do-you-call-her from Rosemount in trouble. Did you not see her? Like the side of a bus already. Somebody was telling me there's a bit of trouble at the bottom of William Street, petrol bombs flying everywhere. Ah yes, and then there's the Troubles. I'm sorry for your Troubles. The capital letter at the start and the s at the end make the difference, not one wake but thousands of them, thousands butchered for a free Ireland or a British state in the northern bit. The head of the body politic severed from the rest. Now that's severe. Capital punishment for being Ireland.

"Thanks Willie."

"I didn't even know she was sick so I didn't. When did she die?"

"She died today. The doctor was attending her but I don't think anybody expected her to die. It was sudden all right."

Willie Henry's big rheumy eyes held me in their respectful gaze. "I was just coming back from the Don Bar there and me blood was up and I was going to give them boys in the police car passing in the street a piece of me mind and then I saw the big black bow on the door there and I says to meself Aw my God, that's Master Coffey's house. Aw my God, don't tell me. I always member you warning me about me two boys and the trouble they were going to get in if I didn't see to them. I always member that, Master. And they're doing all right now so they are. Kevin's down in Doherty's butchers working you know and Hugh's going to get temporary in the Castle Bar coming up to Christmas."

"That's great Willie. I'm glad to hear it."

Father Swindells's voice behind me. "Well now Jeremiah, if you could give me your attention for a moment. I have to be going."

I turned to see the smooth shining face smiling superiorly up into mine. He's forty if he's a day and I'll put on any money the man's never used a razor.

"Thanks for coming Father," I said mustering semblance of gratitude.

"Not at all Jeremiah. Sure what would you expect me to do when one of my parishioners dies? Eh?"

Not many people can make you feel foolish for thanking them but this boy can. And what's this about *my* parishioners? He's only a curate for Christ sake. But he's the school chaplain and that makes him feel important. Charlie Chaplin the weans call him. He was hardly away when Susan and Mairéad went too. I saw them to the front door and when I came back Willie Henry was standing uncertainly at the coffin. I went over to him and joined him staring down at the corpse. The way you do.

"God she's far shook Master. She was a fine looking woman so she was too."

"She was."

"A fine looking woman. Sure I used to see you out the town with her all the time."

I didn't take in what he was saying right. This is what comes of being on autopilot. But now he was gawking over my shoulder and his face was whiter than Maud's. I heard Mammy's voice behind me.

"How are yous all doing?" she was saying and ones were getting up out of their seats to sympathise with her. Willie Henry gripped me by the arm.

"Who's that there in the coffin Master?" he croaked.

"Oh I'm sorry Willie Henry. Did you not know?

I thought you knew. That's Maud Harrigan from next door. We're waking her. She doesn't have anybody."

"Jesus Master, you gave me the wile scare there. Sure I thought it was your moller was dead."

"Would you like to sit down?"

"I'll do that," he said and then whispered in my ear: "You couldn't give me a wee nip of something Master could you? I'm just feeling a bit weak. I'll be all right if I get a wee nip to bring me round."

"I will surely." I said. "Paddy all right?"

"The very thing Master. Just a nip now," demonstrating with finger and thumb wide apart.

When I came back from the scullery Jim Loughery and Seamus White were sitting beside Willie Henry and he was telling them about what happened. They shook hands with me and I smelt the drink off them too. They were laughing and trying to keep straight faces at the same time. Seeing I'd the whiskey in my hand I offered them a drink too.

"I wouldn't say no," said Jim. Plump and happy by nature, eyes like a friendly ferret, looking a bit guilty now because he hadn't even gone to the coffin I'd say.

"Thanks Jeremiah. I'll have a wee one," said Seamus. Always well-cut suit, good tweed too. Some people are like that. Sunday best the seven days. Must be a family thing. Goes back to childhood probably. We used to always wear our best clothes to mass and then change out of them after our breakfast. I looked to see who else was there now. Just Margie McConville. The other women had gone out to the hall with Mammy. I was embarrassed nobody got tea. I was never at a wake where there was no tea. Probably about ten people sitting there in the front room with their tongues hanging out and not one to see to them.

"Margie," I said, "would you fancy a drink? Orange or anything?"

Margie nodded. "I'll have what yous are having. Whiskey'll do fine. I hope it's not watered Jeremiah."

She was smiling away, big rosy face on her. Always up for a bit of crack Margie. Looks like it's the hard core out here in the kitchen.

"Naw, I only bought it the day there so my mother never got at it yet."

She gave a big man's laugh. "Do you mean to tell me she drinks your whiskey and then waters it down to cover her tracks?"

"Naw," I said. "I mean she's the next thing to a prohibitionist."

"Not a dilutionist then?" she said.

"Or illusionist," said Jim.

We were all drinking the whiskey when Mammy came in again and took one look and reversed out. The first two or three sips loosened me. I could feel the tension come off my shoulders and was starting to see on a different level from before the stupidity of the whole thing I was implicated in. For no reason then I thought of Aisling coming to plead with me and her shock when she saw the bow on the door. Or somebody telling her about the blinds being down and her thinking it was Mammy was dead and landing up hoping it might mean a new start for us.

"Somebody told me Maud died intestate," Seamus was saying.

"Where's that?" said Willie Henry.

Margie had her lips tight together to stop the laughing. Her glass was well down already and she was rocking back and forward nearly spilling the rest.

"Aw there's money there," said Seamus. "Straight up. You know she was the daughter of Hoof Hogan."

"Hoof Hogan?" Willie Henry was frowning, eyes half closed as if in deep thought. "I never heard of him now."

"God you must have heard of Hoof Hogan," said Seamus. He left his glass carefully on the empty chair beside him and loosened the top button of his shirt. "Made big money in England so he did and then came home and bought a pub down in Carndonagh. They lived in Troy Park. Hoof had a wile drouth on him from when he came back."

Margie nodded, recovered. "Aye sure he drank most of what he had but he still managed to leave a fair whack behind," she said. "Didn't he marry that Prod from the Waterside what-did-you-call-her? From some English or Welsh family away back wasn't she?"

"Who?" I asked, hearing but not taking it in right. She stood submissively in a gymslip when I strapped her to the cross that time. Soft linen faded to a thread nearly.

"Aw gee," she said screwing up her face, "it's on the tip of me tongue. English I think they were. Their name began with a t and hold on a minute till I think—the first vowel was u or maybe i. Naw, wait a second, wait till I try and remember, I think it started with an m—I'm not sure—but I'm definitely right about the vowel. U it was. Muggeridge … Mulder … Murrick … Hold on, I've got it. Jenkins."

Margie looked round at us all, pleased with herself. "Never turned," she went on. "Let on she did so's she could get her man but then never darkened the door of the chapel after the day of the wedding. She turned queer remember. Do you not remember?"

"You mean …" said Willie Henry, eyewater shining with the scandal of it. "You're not telling me a woman—"

"Ended up sweeping the grass out her front before they put her in the mental. She used to get up in the morning and go out and sweep the grass before even she got her breakfast."

"Howard Hughes is supposed to be like

that," said Jim.

"That's the film man," said Willie Henry. "I didn't know he swept the grass now."

I thought of Aisling again and brought the bottle in and poured out a bit more for everybody.

"Good on you Master," said Willie Henry. "God save Ireland."

"Hoof left school with nothing," said Seamus. "Could hardly write his own name so he couldn't. And then after he got married to your woman they went across the water and he worked as a brickie in London. Never spent a penny if he could help it and ended up a millionaire. This is the nineteen thirties I'm talking about now."

Jim shook his head. "That's a goodun. You'd think I'd have heard of him. Hoof Hogan you say?"

"Hoof Hogan. Rough as a bag of spanners. Dressed like a tramp. He bought a bit of waste ground in London for next to nothing thinking you know it might come in useful sometime and it turned out years after it was wanted for an extra part of a runway for some airport. So one day this boy in a three piece suit comes to the door and offers him half a million for the land. Quarter an acre it was, *less* than quarter an acre. So your man Hoof tells him to go and get lost and he comes back the next week and offers him over a million."

"Handy money," said Jim.

"Handy money all right. This was the nineteen thirties now." Seamus began to smile broadly. He took a sip from his Paddy, looked curiously into the glass and loosened his tie till it hung like a scarf. "But wait till you hear anyway. You won't believe this so you won't. He bought a Bentley."

"That's the car you're talking about?" asked Margie.

"Aye, he bought a new Bentley. Three and a half litre job, Rolls Royce engine, one of the dearest cars going at the time, like a car royalty would have."

"Christ," said Willie Henry scratching at his fork with his free hand. "God forgive me for using the holy name but was that not the car Sean Connery drove in *From Russia with Love* was it not?"

"Not the same car," said Seamus, "but wait

till you hear now what I'm going to tell you. In them days Bentley always did an after sales kind of service where they'd send some top mechanic out to check how the car was performing. So about three months or something after Hoof buys it this Bentley boy arrives at the building site because that's the address he was given you see. So Hoof brings him over to it sitting beside a cement mixer that's churning away. The Bentley's half covered in mud and bits of cement and God knows what else and your man's sort of thrown by all this but anyway he shouts over the noise of the mixer *Tell me, how's she behaving?* And Hoof shouts back at him *Tiptop, tiptop, I'm very pleased with her now. She's a powerful yoke so she is. I was thinking I might put a tow bar on her next week."*

Seamus laughed with his head away back. "I was thinking I might put a tow bar on her next week," he said again. That was in case we hadn't heard it the first time. We all laughed along with him and I was thinking maybe he was going to say it again because I could tell to look at him he wasn't finished but what he said was : "Were you ever in the bar Hoof had in Carndonagh, what's this you call it?"

"I'm not sure. Which one was that?" asked Jim.

"Aw Jesus I'm trying to think. Sure there's so many pubs in the place. There's supposed to be one for every county in Ireland you know."

Margie stifled a shriek, big chest wobbling. "You're not telling me there's thirty-two pubs in Carndonagh."

"At last count," Seamus answered. "I'm just remembering now. The Bore's Head, spelt B-O-R-E."

"He was trying to be funny then?" said Jim.

"He was not. He couldn't spell. He couldn't even write sure, except he learned to write his name on cheques. Naw, the boy that painted the name up, this boy from out the Moville Road I think, wasn't that great of a speller himself. But wait till you hear. Do you know what Hoof said to this crowd of teachers came into the Bore's Head one time the day they got their summer holidays. They were mob happy, is that what you call it?"

"Demob happy?" I offered.

"Demob happy," said Seamus, hitting himself

on the forehead with the palm of his hand. "They were demob happy and one or two of them struck up a song you see after they were in the place about an hour and a half and Hoof comes over to them with a face on him as long as the day and the marra and says *What in under Christ do yous think it is anyway? Are yous in here to have a good time or are yous in here to drink?*"

Willie Henry tried to wipe the tears from his eyes. "God that's a quare wan," he said.

"Are yous in here to have a good time or are yous in here to drink?" Seamus said. He pulled at his tie and it came away and he put it in his jacket pocket.

I got myself into a state that day and beat her sore and she cried and I unstrapped her and took her in my arms. What's wrong with her now with this one Audrey anyway? Didn't she say she was unstable? Okay, let her go and get treatment then.

"Your mother won't mind us drinking?" said Jim.

"Not at all," I told him. She would but I didn't care. To hell with her, her and her phoney show. All the neighbours know she'd no time for Maud. She knows they know but she goes through with it anyway. Would somebody please explain that one.

"Naw but I was saying," said Seamus. "About Maud. I'd say there was money there. There's no surviving relatives is there Jerry?"

"Not that I know of," I said. "My mother always told me there was nobody. I wouldn't be surprised if she left the whole lot to the church you know." Neither I would. She spent that much time in the cathedral the sacristan nearly had to put her out every night when he was locking up. And didn't spend a penny if she could help it, wouldn't even buy a newspaper. *Vera you wouldn't lend me yesterday's Derry Journal would you. There's a death I wanted to see in it.* And you never saw it again. I heard of ones before like that. There was the old doll went about like a pauper down in Wicklow, no, Wexford it was I think, left tens of thousands she'd stashed away under the stairs to the church, relatives up in arms. It's like those people Luther went on about that bought indulgences and paid for a new stained glass window in the chapel as long as their name was put on it. How could I burn in hell if my name's up there in lights behind the altar?

"I wonder what happens if there's no will and there's nobody belonging," Jim said. "You know, when—"

Margie was itching to get her spoke in. "Goes to the state I'd say. The probate office would tell you so they would." Her glass was empty again. She could knock them back all right. She laughed suddenly. "Maybe you're going to come into a fortune Jeremiah."

I looked at her, lightheaded with the drink. I was taking it too fast. Maybe Mammy's the one that's coming into the money. *Don't you be worrying, Maud, if you go before me I'll see to everything. Just you leave aside whatever you think and I'll see to the expenses and all the rest slurp slurp. God that's very good of you Vera.* No, somehow I don't think so. Early this evening you couldn't move but you were tripping over priests coming in and out of the house. That wee busybody Finucane was leading the charge too, he of the twitching curtain. I'd say that boy gets a big bang out of it seeing these upstanding pillars of society wriggling in the pews before they come in and then listening to their litany of secret sins. Makes him feel on a higher plane I suppose. Though what does he do if this guy that's applying for the choirmaster's job tells him behind the curtain that he interferes with boys? What does he do then? How does he explain voting against him if the guy has amazing qualifications? *There's something about him that's not right. What exactly do you mean, Father Finucane? I don't know, I just don't like the cut of his jib.* Code for *Sure you know I'm not allowed to break the seal of confession.*

"I heard of this case down in Galway," said Jim, "where some farmer left everything to the Mormons and the son tried to change the will. He got himself into trouble so he did and ended up not getting a penny."

"Naw," corrected Margie, "it was Roscommon that happened and it was some other crowd. Scientific Church. Or Church of Scientology is it? Naw, not them either." She frowned, put the glass to her head and kept it there for about ten seconds as if she was doing a trick with it on her nose. Then she lowered it and asked: "What is it you call it when somebody changes their will? It was on the TV the other night. Did any of yous see it? Robin Day was interviewing this lawyer about it."

"I saw it," said Seamus. "It's some word like a painkiller or something."

Codicil. When you amend your will. I remember reading about it one time. Rich farmer in Roscommon died leaving every penny plus about a hundred and twenty acres to the Catholic church and the son was fit to be tied. Other farmer down the road Paddy O'Hare or some name like that was the dead spit of the Da so the son went to see him the minute the Da died and asked him to let on to be the Da and make a new will leaving everything to the son himself and O'Hare was to get a quarter of the proceeds. He agreed anyway and they got this solicitor and some witness to come in and they hid the body in the back bedroom so the son could announce the death later on that day. O'Hare's in the bed and the blanket up to his nose and tells the solicitor he's amending his previous will and now wants to leave everything to "my good friend and neighbour Paddy O'Hare." Some scam.

Willie Henry was looking suddenly crestfallen. "Father Swindells'll be getting on to me the next time he sees me," he said.

"How do you mean?" I asked.

"Seeing me with drink in me. Coming into a wake with drink in me. It's not like this is out in the country or something."

"Wise up Willie," said Seamus. "It's none of his business what you do."

Willie Henry's snozzel was starting to run and he wiped it with his knuckles and rubbed the back of his hand discreetly behind the knee of his trousers. "Aw God I doubt it is."

"Don't you be worrying your head about that Willie," said Margie. "The same wee man has his secrets."

"Right?" said Jim.

"Aw aye. And he's not above tapping old ladies for a bit of money to finance his habits either."

"You're telling me that Margie?" Jim was agog. Margie drank from the air, her free hand holding the invisible glass to her lips.

"You don't say," said Willie. "I never knew that now."

"Aw aye. Sure the police stopped him on the lower deck of the bridge one night there at half two in the morning and he was all over the road."

"I heard," said Seamus.

"In his big Cortina," continued Margie. "On the way back from a hard day's night." She laughed loudly and then quickly put her hand up to cover her mouth. "God forgive me," she said, "and Maud lying over there."

"Margie's right," nodded Seamus. "The RUC had a quiet word with the bishop and the bishop had a quiet word with Swindells and it's taxis everywhere now."

"Never got to court?" I asked.

"You're joking," said Seamus.

"I wouldn't have believed it," said Jim.

Neither would I. And it was good to hear. Though you'd have thought somebody in the school would have told me.

"There's a lot of things you wouldn't believe," said Margie. "Did yous not hear about the two oul Quinn sisters from Windsor Terrace?"

"I know them," I said. "Sure they were at the door there a wee while ago. I think they might even be still in the front room now. What about them?"

"Well, that new wee priest in the cathedral started calling at their house once a week. Doing whatever you call it, pastoral visits."

"Father Finucane," said Willie Henry. Eyes gleaming and you couldn't tell to look at him if it was from the gossip or the mucus.

"Was that not a bit often for him to be visiting?" said Seamus.

"It was but you see they'd always left a fiver on the edge of the sideboard beside the door of the kitchen for him to pick up on his way out."

"A fiver a time isn't bad for ten minutes and a blessing," suggested Jim.

"Is that not how Protestants came about?" asked Seamus. "I mean, is that not how it all started?"

"But wait till you hear. Your man Father Finucane just happened to mention to Father Swindells one day about how generous the two oul dolls were and Swindells says to him 'I think maybe you should do the top part of Great James' Street down as far as Prince's Street from now on Father. I'll see to Windsor Terrace.' Pulling rank you see."

"I don't believe it," said Seamus.

"I swear to God," said Margie. "This past I

don't know how long he's been raking in nearly as much as the bishop. And every time after he left the ladies he'd be straight out to the Broomhill House Hotel shooting the whiskeys into him. You can down a fair few drinks for a five pound note so you can and even when he ran out of the readies he was able to sponge off these ones that were hoping he'd put in a good word for their son or daughter coming out of teacher training or whatever. It was nothing ordinary what he drank."

"I mind hearing Irish coffee was his favourite," said Seamus.

"And the rest," nodded Margie. "But you're right about the Irish coffee. Mickey McGriskin told me he saw him putting away seven of them in the one night. And when each new one was set in front of him he'd always say Ah, not only Irish but free."

"I'll drink to that," shouted Willie Henry, eyes more or less closed now, bunged up by phlegm or whatever. "God save Ireland!" He then began a pincer movement, two hands closing in stealthily on his crotch, element of surprise being employed obviously, and quickly pouncing, pressing and possibly nailing whatever was there.

"I heard years ago his mother was one of the Pipers from Slaughtmanus," said Margie. "Did any of yous ever hear tell of them?"

"He who pays the piper calls the tune," said Jim.

We were all laughing when Aisling walked in. I nearly dropped the glass when I saw her. She had on a white mantilla over her long black hair and a dark leather jacket belted at the waist and down below some sort of a grey knee length skirt and black tights and the breath left me. Her face was like a light. She nodded to the wall in front of her and then straight over to the coffin, looked down into it I don't know how long, it wasn't long anyway, and next thing was she turned round and left without looking near me. I got up and my legs nearly went under me. I followed her past mourners whispering in the hall and out to the street. I had no idea what I was going to say to her. She stopped on the footpath at the bottom of our steps and turned to me. Her eyes glistened like seagreen under the streetlight. My head spun. Let her speak. Let her do the talking.

"I thought it was your mother was dead,"

she said, "and I shook hands with her at the door and she told me who she was."

"Did she know who you were?" I asked pointlessly.

"I love you Jeremiah. You know that, don't you? I'm not sleeping."

I opened my mouth to say I'm not sure what but then waited because a bus stopped and sat throbbing very loud in a queue. She was as irresistible as I'd ever seen her. I wanted to hold her and crush her but I stood at a measured distance and when the bus moved on I said: "Will you be going back to Audrey?"

"I can't say I won't."

The firewater was in my head now although I didn't realise it properly and from not knowing what I was going to say I got in a state where I didn't right know what I was saying. "Well make sure she's got the doldos well stocked next time you go up to Belfast" came out. The drink had loosened more than my shoulders.

"What are you talking about?"

"What has she got that I haven't got? Aw I forgot, she's got the doldos."

"You mean dildos? Is it dildos you're thinking of, Jeremiah?"

"Dildo. Doldo. What the hell does it matter what you call it? What's she got that I haven't got?"

"Excuse me Mister Coffey."

I turned round. The two Miss Quinns were waiting to get past me, all aflutter.

"I'm sorry," I said. "I didn't hear you coming."

Two pairs of spectacles flickered nervously. "We were wondering," said one of them, "what time the funeral mass is going to be at."

"It's at ten o'clock".

"Ten o'clock," twittered the other. "That's grand. Some of them are nine and some are eleven."

"And sometimes they're not till twelve," added the first. "Sometimes people have to come over from England and they don't get here till it's late morning."

Aisling was gone.

"But poor Maud had no relations, hadn't she not?" said the other. "Isn't it terrible when you have no one?"

"God have mercy on her soul," they said, one starting on her own, then slowing down so the sister could catch up and they were together on the last three words, heads going like two sparrows.

The street was grey with mist. I looked in the direction she went and saw something shapeless coming towards me. Her coming back? I'm not sleeping, she said. It had been good to see her humble herself and know I could still have her if I wanted. Share her. What was so bad about what she was doing? Was it so bad? Yes it was. Deviant and devious and what's the other thing, promiscuous. Better shot of all that. It would be good to be in the state of grace again anyway, I should never have been out of it. I'd get confession tomorrow before half seven mass after Maud was taken to the cathedral, get confession and clean the slate. The swings and slides in Bull Park dizzied as I turned my head from whoever was coming and tried to think of something to say to the Quinns. Why couldn't they go? I looked down at them and waited for the shape to clear and Aisling to say: "Can I have a word with you in private?"

Big Bill Braddock stepped from out of the murk. "That's a dull old night, isn't it?" he said. He shook my hand and raised his hat to the two Miss Quinns. Addressing me he said: "I was sorry to hear about your neighbour, ah …"

Her name escaped him. I didn't have the presence of mind to supply it. I'd been expecting Aisling.

"Molly. Molly was her name, wasn't it?" he said with assurance. Never a man to lack confidence.

"Maud you mean?" cried one of my companions. "Maud Harrigan."

Bill stared at her and then smiled and murmured: "Ah yes. Maud Harrigan. Of course."

The sisters left us then and I led him to the kitchen. He went to the coffin and I stood dutifully beside him while he blessed himself with something of a flourish and placed a mass card on the dead woman's two piece suit. After praying in a loud whisper May her soul and the souls of all the faithful departed etcetera he turned to see who else was in the room.

Jim, James and Willie Henry acknowledged

him with dumb hostility and Bill looked disapprovingly back at them, having noted the drinks in their hands. Margie was smiling glassily, keeping her own counsel.

"Very sad," Bill said and sat on a chair opposite the others. "All things must pass."

It was at this point that somebody let off, a prolonged squelchy one partly muffled I'd say by a pair of clenched cheeks. The smell came a little later, as it does, and there was no way of knowing for certain who it emanated from, Margie, Seamus, Jim and Willie Henry being seated inscrutably close together, unless you could have had some way of finding out who had had cabbage and baked beans and spiced meatballs too if I'm not mistaken for dinner that day. (My money for what it's worth would have gone on Willie Henry, known to some in Derry by the sobriquet McGillycuddy of the reeks, not to be confused in any shape or form of course with Donough McGillycuddy, direct descendant of Mogh Nuaghad King of Munster and current chieftain of the McGillycuddy of the Reeks clan, educated at Eton and Neuchâtel and now living in Himeville, KwaZulu-Natal, South Africa, according to an article in *The Irish Times* I have here in front of me.)

Neither was there any way of ascertaining whether this rearward breaking of wind was involuntary or carried a message, what I mean is some kind of gesture directed at Bill. Whichever was the case the stink was so bad that it would have made a skunk throw up had one been present. The three male suspects were perfectly unreadable while Margie was staring pointedly at the coffin, lips tight together with controlled I'm not sure what. The thing she was implying by her knowing look was awful of course though not necessarily unthinkable. I suppose Charlie Bradley and Denis McLaughlin would be the ones to ask. I've heard for example that undertakers have to block up all the orifices to stop leaks. It's disgusting when you think about it but I suppose that's the way we're made. If God really exists, and sometimes you have to wonder, you'd think at least He'd have given us a bit of dignity. Temples of the Holy Ghost, isn't that what we're supposed to be? Well, if the Holy Ghost stopped doing whatever it is He does nowadays and thought about it all for a second He might just decide He didn't want His name associated with us.

The air still hadn't cleared when I sat down beside Bill. I had good reason for choosing that particular place to sit because on top of the lingering redolence there was a mood of defiance about and I guessed that one or more of the mourners present had experienced the weight of Bill's authority back in their schooldays. My motives had nothing to do with solidarity I assure you. I simply wanted to keep the proceedings civil. There's nothing as unseemly as a row at a wake, especially if it's reported in the Derry Journal, and I felt a certain responsibility seeing this was my house. So there we sat, Bill and I, facing Jim, Seamus, Margie and Willie Henry. The men had the look, and Margie wasn't far behind, of people that couldn't wait to get started. A growing aggravation was the fact that the four of them were in need of alcoholic replenishment, as I myself was, but there was no way I was going to produce the bottle while Bill was there. The bitter irony about what looked like my support for him was the fact that I too harboured painful memories of his heavy hand, especially in the matter of the Derry Catechism. Who created you and placed you in this world Coffey? God. Why did God create you? To know Him and love Him and serve Him and by that means to gain everlasting life. Now give me the first Commandment. First I am the Lord thy God, Thou...Thou...Thou...Out on the floor Coffey. Out! Next man, give me the first Commandment. First I am the Lord thy God, sir, Thou shalt have no other gods before Me. Good man. Now come over here, Coffey, and give me your hand. Out straight!

If Seamus was well-dressed, which he was, he was put in the shade by the man facing him. Bill's nickname in the school is Waistcoat Willy for he is never seen out of doors without his three piece on. Come winter wind or summer sun it's always the same, the only difference being in extremely sub zero times when he partly covers it with his three-quarter length sheepskin.

"I heard the sound of more trouble when I was on my way here," he said shaking his head. "It's disgraceful what's happening."

"Terrible," I said. Silence from those opposite.

"I blame the parents," he went on. "They ought to know what their children are up to. It's a dereliction of responsibility Jeremiah."

"What do you mean?" said Seamus. "Sure some of the parents are down there pegging stones as well."

Big Bill stared at him wondering if he was serious and then turned to speak to me. "Well if that's the case then all I can say is there's not much hope left for this town."

"What's this Martin Luther King said Master?" Jim said addressing me. "Do you remember what Martin Luther King said? About rioting I'm talking about."

"Rioting is the voice of the unheard," said Margie. "Is that what you're thinking of?"

"That's it," said Jim. "Rioting is the voice of the unheard."

"More like the voice of the unrared," boomed Bill puffing out his waistcoat.

Jim's nostrils flared. "You trying to say the boys out fighting for us weren't rared proper?"

"I'm saying," said Bill exaggerating weary patience, "that far too many mothers in this town are out playing Bingo at night when they should be at home watching their families. That's what I'm saying. And by the way, they're not fighting for me."

"And what about the fathers?" demanded Margie.

"The fathers?" said Bill. "I don't know. You'd need to ask them. Although maybe I can guess."

A line of dilated pupils eyeballed Bill. Count me out here. My eyes were on the floor.

Dangerous silence fell and you had the feeling then that the only thing saving Waistcoat Willy from serious insult was a sense of Catholic decorum. Although some kind of retribution seemed to be at hand wake or no wake. And then, out of the blue, Jim with his fondness for quoting moved the discussion along and so threw Bill an unintended lifeline.

"There's nobody as dangerous," he said, "as the man that has nothing to lose."

Which Bill immediately tossed back into the boat, countering "What about the people who have everything to lose? Or think they have? The ones we're backing into a corner?"

"What are you talking about?" demanded Margie.

I was trying to remember three things at the one time. Where was my whiskey glass, when had I left it out of my hand and was there any in it the time I put it down? In the middle of the frozen silence that followed Margie's question I went out to the scullery and spied my glass with the bottle sitting beside it. I poured a generous glug on top of the thumbnail of whiskey I'd left and put the glass to my head. The heat filled my chest and made up my mind that this was the way to be. I don't know how long I spent out there but whatever length of time it was I still had enough wits about me to leave bottle and glass behind when I went back to the kitchen where Bill was in the middle of advocating a return of the anti-treating league in Ireland as a means of stopping people standing rounds.

"You see," he said, "if there are three in the company then each person ends up taking three, maybe even six, drinks. And let's say you have four people together."

"Got you," said Jim. "Two threes is six and two fours is eight."

"And two fives is ten," added Willie Henry wiping a tear from his cheek. "Jesus that sounds all right to me. And speaking of drink Master." I was the master he was addressing here though of course I wisely ignored him.

"I thought," said Margie, "that the anti-treating league was to stop people standing drinks to spongers. After all, if you're taking your turn to buy your round you're not treating anybody, are you? You're only treating somebody if you buy them a drink without expecting them to buy you one back."

"It's a whatdoyoucallit, a misnomer," agreed Seamus. "Is that what you call it, Margie?"

"The very word," said Margie. "A misnomer. Misnomer's the word."

Bill was now giving me his full attention, determined I think not to let the Greek chorus sidetrack him. It was almost admirable the way he handled the situation but then he's been dealing with unruly classes for more than thirty years. If you can't beat them then pretend they're not there.

"Drink has been the curse of this country, Jeremiah, did you know that?" he said.

I nodded, not trusting myself to speak. This

hasty movement caused the room to spin a little and there and then I made up my mind to keep the head still.

"I really think," he continued, "that the time is ripe for a return to some kind of crusade. They used to have musical evenings away back you know and they'd have young women going round with temperance beverages and cream buns and pastry and the like. Tell me, did you ever hear of the blue ribbon badge?"

I looked straight ahead while he told me about its origins. It was created, he said, by a man called Francis Murphy who took a verse from the Bible as his inspiration. "I can't remember the exact wording," he said, "but I think it went something along the lines of 'Speak to the children of Israel and bid them wear a ribbon of blue as an outward sign of their moderation.'"

"I wonder would he be anything to the Frank Murphy from Buncrana that played for Derry City?" asked Seamus.

"Your man Murphy that played on the left wing you mean?" queried Jim. "Sure he wasn't Frank. He was Stan was he not?"

"It's actually the first instance of the pledge being taken, back around the turn of the century, and it was the only known predecessor of the pioneer pin."

"Aw Jesus, was it that long ago?" said Seamus. "Well it couldn't have been Frank Murphy then."

"Stan," corrected Jim. "Or wait a minute. I tell a lie. I'm thinking of Stan Murphy played the snooker down in the Ancient Order of Hibernians." He waved an arm in the air. "But sure it doesn't matter two damns anyway. The boy your man's on about lived away back."

Your man as Jim impertinently described him then proceeded to tell me about the Catholic Association for the Suppression of Drunkenness, long defunct, and Father Theobald Mathew with one t the great temperance champion and also the reformed drunkard the Venerable Matthew Talbot, Matthew with two ts, who would have been anonymous had it not been for the cords and chains discovered on his body after he collapsed and died in a Dublin street in 1925.

"Self-mortification," Bill explained. At several points during this latest discourse he eyed the mourners opposite with some irritation as all of them except for Willie Henry who was now asleep had become embroiled in a what seemed like a heated argument concerning a brother of Frank Murphy, Mick by name, who at one time had been the best high jumper in the northwest having won money at sports meetings for years from Muff to Malin Head and who after retiring from athletics became known in Buncrana as Mick the taxi or possibly Mick the ambulance. It was this nickname that was the bone of contention, Seamus going with the first named moniker and Margie and Jim, especially Jim, with the second. I could have told them of course that Mick went by both names, the first when he drove a taxi for Buncrana Taxis and the second when he was employed by Carndonagh hospital as an ambulance driver during which time he sometimes still got Mick the taxi even though he hadn't driven a taxi for years. I decided not to do this for two reasons, firstly because Bill was demanding my full attention in an effort obviously to keep his mind off the rabblement opposite and secondly because I wasn't sure how my voice would come out. On that particular matter I had some minutes before decided that I'd be making a beeline for the bottle again the minute Bill left because, although I wasn't in favour of going back to Irish wakes and funerals of old where it was not unknown for mourners to drink all night and then be stretched out in a paralytic state sometimes next to the grave even while interment was taking place, I could see no good reason not to get slaughtered that night and then sleep it off. For this was a wake without bereaved, unique in that regard, and if you couldn't get slaughtered at this one then what one could you get slaughtered at?

"You're wrong," said Seamus to Margie. "It was Mick the taxi. Sure didn't he tell me himself the Sunday he was driving me and Packie and them from the Keg o' Poteen back up to Derry after we missed the last bus when we were down playing the friendly against Clonmany Trojans. And by the way, the anti-treaty league you were asking me about there a minute ago Margie had nothing to do with the other thing. It just so happened some people that were in one were in the other as well. It's like a Venn diagram. Did you ever hear tell of a Venn diagram did you?"

"What's that you're saying?" asked Bill who should have known better.

"It's got two parts that cross over each other," explained Seamus with a trace of condescension. "Like circles. What's the word? Intersect. I did it in Maths at Saint Columb's. Maybe they didn't do it in your day."

"No no," said Bill impatiently. "Not the Venn Diagram. I know all about that of course. I passed Mathematics with distinction. What were you saying about the anti-treaty league?"

"There was actually no such thing in point of fact," continued Seamus. "It wasn't a league as such."

"A misnomer," said Margie.

"Misnomer's the word," agreed Seamus. "The crowd that were against the treaty with England were the Republicans, not the anti-treaty league. And that wasn't actually the name at all in point of fact. What's this now it was?"

The kitchen door opened and a woman from two doors below Aisling's came in. I decided to lie low, figuring she knew where the coffin was. She knelt down and stayed down for ages and then I heard the sobs starting as she was getting up.

Margie put the empty glass that was in her hand sitting under the chair and went over to comfort her, rubbing away at her back as if she was trying to bring her wind up.

"You and Maud were very close, weren't you, Kate?" she said.

Kate. That's who it was, Kate Breslin. Never out of the cathedral, never done bowing and scraping to the priests and putting fresh flowers on the altar, her and Maud and these others ones. I met her a couple of times when I was coming out of Aisling's and from the look on her face at the cut of me I always had the feeling she knew something was going on that wasn't Christian. Well she wouldn't be seeing me again that way.

Between sobs Kate told Margie that she'd been to the Long Tower carnival in the Brandywell showgrounds with Maud last July, just three months ago nearly to the day it was, and the two of them had gone to this fortune teller Madam Esmeralda just for the fun of it and she'd told Maud that she, Maud, would come into an inheritance before the year was out. Margie said "Well maybe the fortune teller was right, Kate, because sure you and I know that Maud's in heaven right now and if that's not coming into her inheritance I don't know what is." I couldn't hear everything Kate said back with all the snivelling but I picked up the not exactly useful information that Madam Esmeralda was actually Sadie Walker from up Creggan Heights and she was in hospital at the minute with a broken hip from the time she got hit by a trailer carrying bricks at the end of Nailor's Row.

"She never seen that one coming," said Jim to nobody in particular. Seamus shook with silent merriment but straightened his face as Kate turned to leave the kitchen. When she was gone Bill returned to the question of the anti-treaty league.

"I think you may be right about that," he said to Seamus. "I don't remember ever reading of any such body. They were known only as the Republicans although of course they later became Fianna Fáil."

A groan from Willie Henry getting geared up, trying to open sleepstuck eyes, slapping his knee. And hark! a voice like thunder spake, the west's awake! the west's awake! "And Fianna failed us!" he shouted. "Dirty scuts!"

"Foiled us," said Seamus nodding. "Fianna foiled us."

"Filed us," added Margie between laughing and serious. "They're supposed to be the Republican party and they filed us away for another day."

"I wouldn't say that," said Bill. "I think there are certain moves being made behind the scenes from Dublin. I think you might soon see Captain O'Neill being summoned to the headmaster's office in Downing Street and given some lines to say."

Willie Henry didn't seem ready to accept this bit of surmising. Looking fiercely into his glass he said: "Dublin? I wouldn't trust that crowd a wankers as far as I'd throw them. Fianna foul!"

"I can't see Wilson or Callaghan or any of them over there doing anything," said Margie. "And what sort of a name is that anyway? Did you ever hear of a prime minister being called captain? What is he the captain of? A cricket team? I remember reading one time he went to Eton. Cricket's what they play there isn't it?"

"He's the captain of a sinking ship," shouted

Willie Henry. A clear case of withdrawal symptoms. Which I also was suffering from but at least I had the wit to keep quiet.

"This place is unreformable," said Margie. "Do you see all this stuff about one man one vote and fair housing and all? The only way this place can be reformed is to hand it over lock stock and barrel to the Free State."

Bill was footering impatiently with his waistcoat buttons and elaborate looking things they were too. "And what would the Free State as you call it do with the Orange Order and the Apprentice Boys and the million Protestants that are afraid of Rome rule?"

Willie Henry came out fighting. "What do you mean Rome rule?" he demanded.

"Aye, what do you mean Rome rule?" said Margie. "That's the kind of language Carson used. And Craig and Basil Brooke and the whole rogue's galley of them."

"Gallery," I said impulsively.

"What?" shouted Willie Henry, picking distractedly at hardened phlegm from the inside corner of one eye and dislodging what looked to me like red clots.

"Gallery," I repeated and then closed my eyes, sorry I'd spoken. The hard g at the start of the word had caused a sharp pain to shoot across my forehead twice in quick succession.

"Margie's right," said Seamus emphatically. "Rogue's galley's what they are. Because they're all going to go down with the ship so they are."

Bill shook his head reprovingly. "Tell me this now," he said. "Just tell me this. How would you feel if you were a Protestant being handed over to the Republic of Ireland and wanting to marry a Catholic? Eh? You'd have to promise to change your religion and bring up any children you might have in the Catholic faith. Would you not think your religion was being forced into extinction?"

"And what's wrong with that?" said Jim. "Weren't the Planters brought in here by the English to keep the Catholics down? And aren't these Prods living here now all from Planters? And didn't their religion start in the first place from that goat Henry not getting a divorce from the pope?"

"The Protestants that are against the marchers didn't come in with the Planters you know," said Bill in a voice normally reserved for the backward row. "The Plantation of Ulster happened over three hundred years ago. What Protestants see now is their birthright being threatened. They know that a lot of the people out there marching are the children or grandchildren of migrants from over the border. There's nothing black and white here. And if I may say so, a little bit of empathy wouldn't go amiss."

The looks on the faces opposite were thunder dark. Whatever empathy is it can go to hell, they said. And suddenly the air seemed to have got thinner. Whether this was to do with my state of mind and body or the heightened feelings in the room or the fact that the kitchen window couldn't be opened because it had been painted so many times or maybe even all three of the aforementioned I'm not sure. I could always have gone and opened the back door I suppose but then cold air might have knocked me out and anyway the two wandering black cats from Majella Doherty's would have taken the open door as an invitation and I couldn't have that. This was nothing to do with superstition because I'm not superstitious or it being in bad taste, there being a wake in progress, but because Milly and Molly, for those were their names, always had a sweet smell about them that brought decomposing rats to mind. Options being limited to sitting doing nothing therefore I sat doing nothing if you can call listening doing nothing.

"It was Michael Collins," said Seamus, "that struck the first blow against the British Empire. Did you know that?"

I turned my head slowly to look at him feeling vaguely grateful. Disadvantaged by the whiskey though I was I could still sense what he was at. He was trying to steer the conversation away from the rocky road to Dublin. Or so it seemed to me anyway.

"Aye, that's true," nodded Jim. "And with a bit of luck this wee town of ours could finish them off."

"What do they say?" said Braddock carefully ignoring Jim's remark. "The sun never sets on the British Empire?"

"That's because it doesn't trust them in the dark," said Margie. This remark brought a smile to Big Bill's face, a rare occurrence as he's a forbidding sort of git most of the time, and loud laughter from all others present except myself for reasons that shouldn't need explaining here.

"England's nothing but a pup," said Seamus. "A mongrel pup too."

"A bastard pup," added Willie Henry passionately. There was a look about him now that made me worry. This man was in need of a drink and there was no telling what he might end up saying or doing.

"Oh dear," said Margie. "Maybe we shouldn't be using language like that, showing disrespect for Maud that's lying there."

"Not at all," Seamus reassured her. "Maud knows nothing that's going on here now. Sure the soul only stays in the body three hours and then after that it's in heaven."

"Or the other place," Willie Henry said clawing at his front of his trousers like there was something at him again or maybe it was the nerves. Ready for the hills anyway.

He looked up then for a reaction and, receiving none, held out his glass plaintively. Plaintiffly. This latter gesture was directed at me of course but I resolutely ignored it even though I had a strong idea how dire his state was. I felt sorry for him, as I did for myself, but there was no way the drink was coming out again till that bastard

Braddock left.

    Mister Abel Doak prosecuting stated that the defendant William Henry McGillycuddy, who had earlier made a submission to the court requesting that he be referred to as the plaintiff, had been intoxicated when he trashed and subsequently dismantled the wakehouse in Marlborough Terrace (the only items left intact being the softwood casket and its contents, viz., the earthly remains of one Maud Abilene Harrigan) yet by his own admission was not so intoxicated that he was unaware of what he was doing. Defending, Mister Jules Bernestock made the point that all the defendant William Henry McGillycuddy, hereinafter hopefully called 'the plaintiff', had been seeking was one miserly shot of Paddy, being still in a badly shaken state after having encountered what he took to be a corpse welcoming him to the wake. "To quote the plaintiff," said Mr Bernestock consulting his notes, "*I was just after saying a Hail Holy Queeng in the corphouse standing looking down into the face of the poor dead woman when I turned round and there she was fornenst me saying 'It was wile good of you to come Willie.'* (At this point Mister Justice

Tickel van Rumpole showed commendable Dutch courage in facing down a rumbustious courtroom, threatening to have the place cleared forthwith if the merriment did not cease, on foot of which threat order incrementally returned to the proceedings.) *And all I got to bring me round were two nips of Paddy you could hardly see."*

Mister Justice van Rumpole, on occasion sipping from a hipflask which transparently contained water-coloured liquid, then asked Mr Bernestock to clarify Mr McGillycuddy's request to be dealt with as a plaintiff. Mr Bernestock thereupon came out with a whole load of stuff in Latin to support the legal argument that a defendant can in certain cases, one of which this clearly was, ask the court to declare him a plaintiff. Mr Justice van Rumpole accepted that as it had earlier been established that Mister Jeremiah Coffey the householder, hereinafter called 'the possessor', had been aware of Mr McGillicuddy's distressed state and therefore (it could be argued) was partly culpable for the Marlborough Terrace premises being effectively removed from future ordnance survey maps. "Yet," he concluded, "although it may well be that there was equal fault on both sides, the burden is always placed on the plaintiff, and the cause of the possessor is preferred. How and ever this is a matter for another court thank Christ. Next case please. Now where did that flask go?"

"Tell us this," Willie Henry went on, lowering the glass glumly. "One of the masters would know the answer to this one. If Maud, God have mercy on her almighty soul, is in heaven this minute, do yeez think she would know what's going to happen? Here in Derry like? Does she know how it's all going to turn out does she? What I'm saying is, for an example now, could she tell you the date Ireland would be free could she?"

"That's a good question," said Margie thoughtfully. "I think there's something in the Bible about that. Even somebody simple, God bless the mark, would know as much as Einstein once they got to heaven. I don't know about predicting the future though."

"Or Shakespeare," said Jim. "Maud's there with God now and He'd be telling her everything."

"Naw, that's wrong," said Seamus. "It's like the barrel and the thimble. If you're like a thimble in this world then you'll be a thimble in the next one too. A thimble can only hold so much. That's the thing you see."

Willie Henry wasn't having this. "No harm to you, Seamus, but you're ignorant, if you don't mind me saying, no harm to you. It was the masters here I was asking."

"Did you hear that, Seamus?" said Margie, shoulders going. "You're a thimble."

"That's an interesting point you've brought up," responded Bill, blinking owlishly in Seamus's direction while doggedly avoiding Willie Henry's gaze, "about the relativity of knowledge."

There then followed a partly political broadcast by and on behalf of Big Bill Braddock about happiness and knowledge and moderation and seeing through a glass darkly and seeing through a glass brightly and Daniel O'Connell the Liberator and Saints Gregory and Sylvester and the Little Flower and plenty more not to mention the Venerable Seraphim of Sarov or maybe the Venerable Sarov of Seraphim it was. What he seemed to be saying leaving aside the politics was: *Our Maud who art in heaven, hollow be thy brain. Thou will be dumb in heaven as you were on earth.* The broadcast went on for some time without so much as a heckle and partway through Willie Henry lost interest and returned to sleep. When it was as clear as the nose on your face that Bill had finished and wasn't just drawing breath Jim shook himself with the air of a man about to come out for round two.

"You mentioned Daniel O'Connell there," he said. "Great patriot and all. Do you want to know what a lot of the people away down in Kerry say about him?"

"What?" asked Bill guardedly.

"That when he was going round liberating Ireland you couldn't throw a stick over the wall of a poorhouse without hitting one of his bastards."

Bill winced but quickly rallied. "Protestant propaganda put about at the time and the Republicans got into bed with them so to speak."

"I don't think the Republicans were the ones getting into bed with housemaids now so to speak," said Margie smiling sweetly.

"There's no smoke without fire," added Seamus darkly.

Bill took a deep breath and launched into a

robust defence of the Liberator. "The fire in this case was lit by an unholy alliance of Planters and warmongers." he explained. "The Planters hated him because he fought for Catholic emancipation and the Republicans hated him because he said violence was stupid and wrong."

"Except when he was the one doing it himself," shouted Willie Henry, the west having suddenly wakened up again. "Didn't he shoot Fred Astaire didn't he?"

A mystified silence followed while the rest of us pondered this claim, wondering just what to make of it, until it was clarified by Bill. "You may be thinking," he said, "of John d'Esterre, a member of Dublin corporation. O'Connell criticised the corporation for being anti-Catholic and this man d'Esterre challenged him to a gun duel. O'Connell won and d'Esterre died from his injuries."

"Well there you are then," said Seamus, stroking his stomach with satisfaction and sticking his thumbs inside the belt of his trousers. "Political violence. The very thing he was death on himself."

"Aye," seconded Willie Henry, "there you are, the very thing I was after saying. Except when he was doing it himself."

"Stupid and wrong? Is that what the oul goat said is it? Well that's a goodun," cried Jim, eyeing Bill with mild venom. "So Michael Collins was stupid and wrong then? If it hadn't a been for Michael Collins the British would still be here the day so they would."

"But they are still here," returned Bill. "And what exactly was the result of all those killings he organised down there? A confessional state. A confessional state where the Irish army attends mass clicking their heels and armed to the teeth."

The room was seething with insurrection now, the only ones out of it being me and Maud. My pressing need at that particular time was to empty my bladder but I had a feeling that if I stood up I would fall down so I sat tight if that's the right word.

"So do nothing then?" demanded Seamus. "Is that what you're saying? What are you anyway? An Ulster Unionist? A Paisleyite?"

Bill's cheeks flapped like a flibbering jib and his waistcoat swelled fit to burst threatening to send buffalo hoof buttons, for that indeed was what they were made of—I had this from Bill himself at the last staff do in the Castle Inn—ricocheting round the room like shrapnel. It was at this parlous juncture that Father Hourigan chose to make his entrance. The Reverend Doctor Xavier Hourigan no less, cathedral administrator, chairman of three school boards—including mine God help me—and scourge of slacking teachers in the parish of Saint Eugene. I'm tempted to tell you that I was never as glad to see anybody in my life but since that would be a lie I'll just say I was mighty relieved that a blazing row had been nipped in the bud. I jumped to my feet like a squaddie when the sergeant comes in and the room began to swim in front of me butterfly style. In an instinctive attempt to remain upright I used what is known in the States as the two-handed greeting—I've seen politicians in their presidential campaigns use it as a way of gaining support for their cause, Richard Nixon and George Wallace being two examples that come to mind at this minute in time.

    I suppose I should explain here. The two-handed greeting is a vigorous handshake with the right hand while grasping the other person's upper arm with the left. Support your local drunk. I was bit free with him I grant you, a bit touchy feely considering this was a man who lived by certain immutable tenets on the matter of physical contact but what can you do, it was either hold on to his arm or fall by the wayside. The cleric drew back like a scalded cat, then recovered his poise somewhat and gave me a long searching look down the length of his nose. Regular old trooper, never put out for too long. On the matter of his nose by the way. The hairs that sprout from it like curly weeds are grey as befits a man of his age but look at his hair, I mean to say the hair on his head. It's as black as your boot. So there, what does that tell you? Vanity. That's what I'm talking about. Vanity pure and simple.

    He glanced round the rest of the company and nodded stiffly, reserving a greeting of sorts for Big Bill Braddock who, though still steaming from his recent altercation with the rebels, managed a good to see you Father in return. The priest then moved with great gravitas towards the coffin and as he did so a vicious stab at the base of the bladder told me how desperate I was to do my number one so taking advantage of the fact that Hourigan temporarily had his back to me and that I now found myself in a standing position I made my way carefully to the bathroom dislodging and miraculously catching and then replacing a flying duck in the process. Pointless things these ducks. Never liked them. You'd be better with a blank wall. Once locked in I gripped the wash-hand basin and slumped back on the toilet seat. I hadn't done a pee sitting down since I was about three or whatever but I thought Why not? If I do it standing up half of it will probably end up on the floor so I may as well do it where I am. It stung a bit at the start but when I was partway through I was thinking, Christ, this is as good as sex nearly, this is like a bloody orgasm so it is, and when I got near the end I fixed my eyes on a particular spot on the wall hoping the focus would help me to get the best I could out of it.

    And that was the moment I saw him doing the same old tricks. I don't exactly know what class of an insect he is but he's been there for years. If it wasn't the same boy then it had to be one of his offspring though if that was the case it was very strange indeed because there's never been more than a day between his death and the appearance of his fully grown replica.

    But there he was anyway, swinging his way down the wall, for all the world as if he was abseiling only without the props, enjoying I would say stunning aerial views of the wash-hand basin and bath and scuffed lino and me on the toilet seat, swinging with gay abandon and what do you call it, consummate skill. The thing is, he's always there, day in day out, no winter break, he's not one of these ones that disappear into a hairline in the wall to hibernate, no, this boy's at it all seasons, abseiling away there on that part to my right above the bath, always the same place too. I watch him a lot of times I'm doing my number two when I've forgotten to bring in the newspaper. It used to be a bit of crack watching him till he started this other trick he has of jumping about like a bed bug and then disappearing so you haven't a clue where he's got to, if he's maybe in your hair or somewhere worse. Those times I felt like waiting for him to reappear so I could kill him with the toilet brush but he never did and anyway his patch is just that bit out of reach when you're sitting down and you wouldn't know what would happen if you came off the toilet seat in the middle of it all to clock him one. It's as if he knows you're at a disadvantage and he's teasing you. And then when you've got your business finished and the toilet flushed and your trousers back on he's gone of course. He just goes. It's as if he only comes out when certain smells are there.

Anyway this particular night of the wake I was sitting on the bowl doing the last dregs watching the swinging pendulum kind of descent he does and I suddenly realised I'd been feeling hot and prickly for a while and then it came to me I still had my trousers on. Well fuck me, I thought, and then I said to hell with it, I'm nearly finished anyway. So I put my mind to enjoying the rest of it but the enjoyment was greatly diminished, nonexistent if I'm being completely truthful, because I was thinking that after I finished I should strictly speaking soak my lower half in the bath, a manoeuvre that has never appealed to me even sober, and then get magically dried with the wee hand towel Mammy had left in the bathroom and change from the waist down.

Imagine only leaving a hand towel and all those people coming in. She'd shame you.

The logistics involved in the washing and drying and changing seemed too impractical if not impossible to consider seriously since all my clean clothes were upstairs and to get there minus trousers and underpants and with only a small hand towel held in front of me would present some difficulty. I had a fleeting image of me charging through the hall and streaking past stunned mourners up the stairs like Tarzan. And to add to the gravity of the situation the wakeroom would be on my route of course which meant I'd have to pass Hourigan whom I could hear at that very minute holding forth in his pulpit voice on what drink was doing to family life in Derry. I therefore made up my mind on no account to leave the bathroom until the priest had gone.

The way I felt just then I wouldn't have minded downing the rest of that Paddy and the thought of sitting on the toilet seat with the bottle for company held a certain appeal. And the thought grew until it became a preoccupation until it in turn became like an obsession and I was actively planning on making a quick sortie to the scullery which after all was only one door away when I heard women's voices on the other side of that very door which, in case I haven't explained the geography right, is where the scullery actually is. Mammy's was one of them and I was able to extrapolate from the mostly rubbish they were talking that they were making tea and opening packets of spring-sprongs, also known as coconut creams.

So it was a case of sitting it out. I could live with that, I thought, though the wet clothes were an irritation and some had got through to my socks and shoes. Urine I remembered from a bar quiz was ninety-five percent water, which goes to show that there's no such thing as useless knowledge, but I couldn't remember what the other five percent was and then it came to me. Leonora the sister-in-law, disaster if ever there was one, going on about the causes of nappy rash and though I'd made a point of not listening to a word she was saying some of it must have percolated because it was then I made up my mind to take the thing by the scruff of the neck. So with only two minor falls one of which occasioned a split lower lip I got my Y-fronts and trousers and shoes and socks off and dabbed myself dry with the hand towel which I then returned carefully to the side of the bath. Next up was what to wear. I scanned the bathroom and could see nothing but a flowered apron of Mammy's drying on the convector heater.

"Jeremiah!"

Mammy. Say nothing. If I don't answer she won't know I'm here.

"Jeremiah, are you all right?"

Don't weaken.

"Jeremiah, it's you in there, isn't it?"

On the other hand if I don't answer she might think I'm lying unconscious and then she'll get someone to force the door and then what? What will all those women think when they see the bottom half of me?

"I'll be out in a minute," I called as matter-of-factly as I could. "Tell me, is Father Hourigan still there? In the wake room?" I tried to make these last two questions sound airy as if I wouldn't have minded a chat with him though it didn't really matter that much but I don't think Mammy bought it.

"What do you want to know that for?" she shouted. "What does he want to know that for?" She could only have been directing the second question to the other women in the scullery. Two responses came, the first of which was: "What does he want to know what for?" and the other: "Here, I'll go and see if I can get him." Stupid woman whoever she was. Did she think I wanted the last rites or what?

A brainscalding pause that went on for anything up to five minutes, and then: "He's away out the door. He left there a minute ago." Blessed be God. Blessed be His Holy name. Blessed be Jesus Christ true God and true man.

To add to the relief I remembered that weeks ago I'd stuffed a Woolworth's bag containing a pyjama bottom with dried in dreams on it into a next to inaccessible space between the bath and the wall. I'll really have to buy a washing machine, I thought as I reached my hand in and dragged out the dusty bag slightly skinning my knuckles in the process. Least of my worries. The pyjamas were quite stiff in places but apart from that, perfect. I replaced them with my trousers, underpants and socks and returned the bag to its hiding place. My coordination wasn't the best because when I withdrew my hand this time the knuckles were bleeding. But no pain so that was all right.

I did my best to sail breezily past the women in the scullery with a civil Hi, ladies. I'm not sure if it came off but nobody passed any remarks. This gave me the confidence I needed for my entrance into the wake room. What the hell, I reckoned, the worst that people can say is that I'm dropping a heavy hint about the late hour without actually telling them to get out.

"And where is Charles De Gaulle now?" demanded Bill.

"In the easy palace," answered Willie Henry.

"Exactly," nodded Bill without turning a hair. "He's sitting pretty in the Élysée Palace. So what exactly," he continued, "did the student revolt, th-th-th-the streetmongering achieve? Exactly what did it achieve?"

"Sweet damn all," shouted Willie Henry.

"Exactly," said Bill. "It achieved nothing. But mind your language sir. The deceased is lying next to you. Sorry, what's her name?"

"Maud Abeline," spluttered Margie. "Maud Abeline Harrigan."

Bill nodded gratefully. "An unusual name. And by the way, don't expect any help from Europe when it comes to achieving human rights in this part of Ireland. Europe hasn't exactly rushed to help the people of Czechoslovakia and Yugoslavia in their hour of need."

Margie was giving my pyjama bottoms the once-over and I wasn't happy about the expression on her face. Undisguised glee I think would cover it. I remembered then that I hadn't any underpants on and heart in mouth I sneaked a look down to see if I was decent. Nothing in sight. I decided I'd be all right as long as I didn't move. What the future held was something else. Truth to tell, I was in God's hands.

"Too right," said Seamus. "But can anybody tell me what America's doing? Why are they sitting there doing nothing when people out in those places are getting slaughtered? The land of the free. Isn't that what they call themselves?"

"You wouldn't happen to have any more whiskey out there Master would you? I wouldn't say no to a wee nip."

Realising that I was the master in question I gazed raptly at the part of the floor visible between my legs and was horrified to see that a space had opened up in my fly and was widening even as I gazed. For this to happen in front of human remains and in company which included one female, broadminded though she clearly was, was bad enough but I was conscious that three other women would be emerging from the scullery any minute with tea, spring-sprongs and sandwiches. Or four was it? Hard to remember. I quickly crossed my legs.

"America's too busy killing thousands of Vietnamese just so they can save face," explained Bill.

"Right, there's another thing. What are they doing out there anyway?" said Jim. "Is that not the stupidest war ever was?"

"It's about money," said Bill. "It's a fraud in fact. This thing stopped being about communism a long time ago. It's about arms companies lining their pockets and then giving millions to the Democrats so they can be re-elected. Or the Republicans as you'll see next month."

"They're all a crowd of bastards!" shouted

Willie Henry.

Nothing daunted Bill proceeded with his analysis:

"That's why John Kennedy was assassinated of course. And Bobby. He was planning to pull out just like his brother was."

"That's what I always thought," said Seamus. "It's a scandal when you think about it. I've a cousin from Ohio was killed in that Tet offensive at the start of the year and his whole family think he died for his country."

"Well so he did," said Bill. "He died fighting for big business. That's what America is, big business. How would you put it? Uncle Sam plc? A lot of the boys that aren't conscripted join up because they think they're answering their country's call."

"Stars in their eyes," said Margie. "Fifty."

"Well, they're fed this pup about the American dream from first grade and a fair percentage never grow out of it," continued Bill, directing his attention to Seamus and Jim as if Margie hadn't opened her mouth. "And do you know that many of them actually think the people who drew up their constitution were inspired by God."

"Like the boys that writ the bible." This interjection from Willie Henry. Bill cast a tolerant look in his general direction.

"It's not going to last, is it?" asked Jim. What was this anyway? They'd been getting ready to drink Bill's blood before the priest came in and now it was all sweetness and light. I wasn't exactly in the right condition to get to the bottom of the new dispensation and of course I'd missed a few instalments but it nearly seemed in my tender state of mind as if Hourigan had been maybe sent in by God Himself. For behold, every mountain and hill shall be made low and the something shall be made straight? And the something something smooth?

"What's not going to last?" said Bill. "The war?"

"No, I mean America," said Jim. "Sure it's an empire isn't it? And empires all end, right?"

Bill was in his element all right. I saw him throw one or two darting looks at my pyjama bottoms but he was on a roll and not inclined to be sidetracked. "It is. It's been an empire for well over a hundred years now and as for lasting I'd give it another couple of hundred years at most. No, you have to remember that many of the founding fathers picked up this notion called manifest destiny. That meant they thought they'd got approval from God Himself to invade any country they wanted if it was for America's good. And it's still there. It's actually racist in origin you know. This is what makes them so dangerous. It's the sense of entitlement that they have."

The scullery door swung open and there was Mammy with a steaming teapot in one hand and a plate of Madeira in the other. I didn't buy Madeira. Somebody must have brought it in. The rest of the caterers, four in number, stood in a row behind her carrying trays of cups and saucers, milk and sugar and platefuls of spring-sprongs and sandwiches. I actually don't know what they'd been at out in the scullery all that time unless it takes five women to make a pot of tea. Because every single salad sandwich had been prepared by me and it was me that bought the spring-sprongs in Strains. Bonding probably, that's what women do isn't it? Strange mysterious people, I'll never understand them. Hurrying me to tighten the bonds and her still wet from the shower that time and the halter neck plastered to her skin and the deep dark hollows underneath, mother of God, and the Flower Duet playing above the beating, louder than her squeals even.

And then followed the most revolting five minutes I've ever spent in Mammy's company. "Och sure you'll take another sandwich will you not Seamus? You will surely. And how are your ones all doing anyway? That's great. How's your mother keeping, Margie? Isn't that great now. She went through a bad time there for a while didn't she? God knows you never know what's round the corner. Sure look at Maud. Will you not have a coconut cream Mister Braddock? Jeremiah got them fresh down in Strain's this evening there. Och go on would you, have one. And how're you keeping, Jim? That's the nicest wee girl you have. Sure I saw her at the First Communions last May there. Shirley Temple I says to Maud, the spit of Shirley Temple in that picture she was in, Dimples wasn't it? Are you taking tea Jeremiah? Are you sure it won't keep you from sleeping now? Jeremiah usually doesn't drink tea at night for fear it'll. All right, if you want, son. It's light enough anyway."

"We were just talking about America there Missus Coffey," said Margie. "Do you think they'd ever put a good word in for us with Westminster? The Catholics I mean."

Mammy didn't understand the question. "How do you mean? Here Nellie, you wouldn't take this pot of tea and cake into the front room would you? Give Maeve that plate of biscuits, sure she'll carry that, won't you, Maeve? Can yeez manage now? What way are you talking about, Margie? I don't exactly follow you."

"Naw, it's just we were on about America there and I was thinking they might be able to influence England you know to give us equal rights here."

Mammy's face darkened. "The first thing I'd like to see is that gang of hooligans off the streets. Sure they're destroying the town so they are. I've a nephew a Jesuit priest out in America and he's coming here next week with his sister a nun in charge of a big school in New York and his niece going on to be a doctor. They're all coming and God knows what they're going to think."

"But they love the Irish don't they?" persisted Margie. "And there's millions of Irish out there would support us."

"Do you really think so?" said Mammy. "When they see on the TV what that crowd down the town's doing I don't think they'd support anything so I don't. Honest to God I don't."

"I know one thing," said Seamus. "The American women would fall over themselves to get an Irishman even if he'd two heads on him. That's a fact."

Mammy looked gravely at him. "I don't know where you heard that from now Seamus."

"Aw it's true," said Jim. "Sure I read about this Yankee widow woman was on a cruise round the Cape of Good Hope one time and she got to talking to this shifty looking wee Corkman was on his own and she says to him *Why did you decide to come on the cruise then?* And he says to her *Well the fact is ma'am I'm on the run. Escaped from prison there last week.* And she says *Oh really? And what were you in prison for if you don't mind me asking?* And he says *I killed me wife with a hatchet so I did and I sent the pieces in a parcel to her mother*. And she says *Oh, so you're single then."*

Everybody laughed except me and Mammy, me because I needed to be careful about making sudden movements on account of both my head and the other thing and Mammy because she has no sense of humour and she's stupid. Even Bill laughed, nearly spilled the tea he was laughing that much. You wouldn't have believed he was the same man walked in the door. Mammy stood there a bit baffled but the same woman's never at a loss for long.

"There's only one man we can trust to do anything," she said, "and that's Eddie McAteer. If people would listen to him then we might get something done."

Willie Henry spoke up. "Eamonn McCann said on the TV he's...what's this he said he is?"

"Who? McAteer?" said Margie. "Middle-aged, middle-class and middle of the road."

Mammy looked down at her, waiting for more and when it didn't come she said "And what's wrong with that? Sure that's the kind of man we need."

"Naw Margie," said Jim. "McCann was talking

about the Derry Citizens' Action Committee. John Hume and them. Eddie McAteer and the Nationalist party's finished Missus Coffey."

"The Nationalist party's finished, long live the Nationalist party," Seamus said smiling away to himself.

Big Bill Braddock had been chewing at the bit during this political chat and then he spoke or maybe it should be spake: "You have two distinct entities here. The Action Committee are Catholic reformers and McCann's people are Marxist revolutionaries. Most people don't trust Marxism because they've a feeling it only makes sense in small groups, you know, like communes and the like. So these revolutionaries are going about in a kind of heroic expectation. Some of them are probably prepared to die even. Violence is McCann's only chance actually, violence done by the state against the people."

"Sure isn't that how Gandhi got the British out of India?" said Margie.

"Aye but Gandhi was organised," said Jim. "McCann's crowd can't even agree what time to start a meeting at."

"They couldn't run a bath," shouted Willie Henry rocking back and forward. And emboldened by what he took to be the prevailing mood he added "Or a piss-up in a brewery." He looked round for a seconder and finding none must have decided he hadn't made his point properly. "Or a whatdoyecallit in a hoorhouse." He smiled then, pleased I think at his self-restraint. We all knew what a whatdoyecallit was but I for one was grateful that the word hadn't been made flesh.

Mammy went rigid. "Willie Henry," she said and her voice was scarcely a whisper, "Do you not know you're in a corphouse now? Have you no respect? That's what the drink does!"

Her head swivelled till she had me in her sights. "And who was it gave it to you? I think I can guess." The last lot of words came out in fragments as if they'd about ten syllables each because, and don't ask me how I knew but I did even though at this stage I was fixed on the flying ducks, she had noticed my bottom half. And she was opening her mouth to say I know not what when Willie Henry spoke fidgeting nervously at his fork with the two hands. "I'm wile sorry

Missus Coffey. I didn't mean any disrespect so I didn't, honest to God."

She stared at him and blinked and then put her hand on the doorknob. "I must help the girls in there. They'll be wanting help I think." She threw me one last scalding look and was gone.

+++++

Radio 3 playing low, soft and low. What is it, chamber music? Anything that brings sleep will do. Jesus what a night and still not shot of her. Lying down there in a box in the dark in the corner, still occupying our kitchen, *our* kitchen, still controlling the agenda and her stiff as a board. Half six tomorrow evening we'll, Charlie Bradley and Denis McLaughlin that is, will bring her, me and Charlie Bradley and Denis McLaughlin, morticians, will bring her to the cathedral for her overnight stay, bed and board, breakfast not included. She should feel at home there right next to the altar where her and Kate and friends dusted and fussed at the flowers and the rest. Tulips were the ones she always tried to get up, you'd have thought they were the only flower there was. And the colours, green, cream, orange, white, red, every colour you could think of nearly except. Blue was it? Blue I think. I never remember seeing blue. Where did she get them when they weren't growing here? I've seen them standing up there proud and erect all times of the year. Imports from Holland? When it's spring again I'll bring again tulips from Amsterdam. Not any more she won't.

What's that they're playing now? Christ I don't believe it. It is. It's the fucking Flower Duet. I don't want to hear it. I need to sleep. Well, maybe just a wee bit, maybe just a minute.

> *Under the dense canopy*
> *Where the white jasmine*
> *Blends with the rose*
> *On the flowering bank,*
> *Laughing at the morning*
> *Come, let us drift down together,*
> *Let us gently glide along*
> *With the enchanting flow*
> *Of the fleeing current*
> *On the rippling surface.*
> *With a lazy hand*
> *Let us reach the shore.*

Her eyes were shining now. "Forget about all the other things. I love you."

"And I love you too."

"Sleep," she said. She fondled my face and shoulders and when the alarm went off her hands were still on me.

Mellifluously a voice told the story of the music. Nilakantha the Brahmin priest goes from his home to attend a gathering of the faithful and leaves behind his daughter Lakme and her slave girl Millika. The two maidens go off hand in hand towards a river in search of blue lotus flowers. As they approach the water they disrobe and Lakme removes her jewellery and leaves it on a bench.

The music came again, sinful, sinuous, insinuating, sin through every orifice. She stood in front of me in diamond drop earrings, Jesus, diamond drop earrings and hot pants, nothing else, turquoise blue.

The bed wasn't the best and I was nervous. Understandable of course. I didn't mind Maud lying one flight down in the corner of the kitchen up to her eyes in mass cards because she could hear nothing, her three hours were up and her soul gone west. An empty shell. No, it was the living I was thinking of, the reverent mother in there in the next room whispering away at her novenas, ear cocked, every sound in her sights. I knew I should be careful but time was short: the song only lasted five minutes, six minutes max depending who was performing. So caution to the winds I went for it, squeezing it all into the four and a half minutes or whatever it was, me and the bolster as if there was no tomorrow. Or rather, knowing there was tomorrow and tomorrow was the start of the dry season. Because the minute we'd parked Maud over at the head of the women's aisle for the night and got through the prayers for the happy repose etcetera I'd be heading for wee Father Finucane behind the curtain and clearing out the clutter with him God help me as my go-between. Between me and my Maker. For I am resolved with the help of Thy holy grace never more to offend Thee but to amend my life Amen. Oh yeah? Yeah, this time it's for real. One last heave and that's it. She wasn't whispering the novenas anymore. No, when she got to Saint Jude patron of hopeless cases she was nearly shouting them.

+++++

This is the last will and testament of Maud Abilene Harrigan. I hereby revoke all previous wills and testamentary dispositions made by me. I appoint my good neighbour Veronica Coffey as executor of this will and direct her to pay my just debts, funeral and testamentary expenses.

To his lordship Most Reverend Doctor Neil Farren, Bishop of Derry, I leave twenty-seven acres and three roods of land, my four local residences and the sum of £95,000.00 stg (ninety-five thousand pounds sterling). For the upkeep of the altar and future renovations to Saint Eugene's cathedral I leave £750,000.00 stg (seven hundred and fifty thousand pounds sterling). To my good neighbour and executor Veronica Coffey I leave my terra-cotta Child of Prague, three ceramic wild ducks and all other wall furnishings in my Marlborough Terrace home.

The residue and remainder of my properties of any nature and description and wherever situated I leave in five equal shares between the order of the Poor Sisters of Michael the Archangel and the four priests of the parish of Saint Eugene's, viz., the

Reverend Doctor Xavier Hourigan and Fathers Clarence Swindells, Benjamin Finucane and Frank Callanan.

SIGNATORIES: Father Thaddeus Updegrave and Sister Henry Antony of the no longer Poor Sisters of Michael the Archangel.

+++++

Let me get this straight. She left every penny to the church and they don't have to lift a finger except to sign the cheques and rake in the readies. It's not as if they're short of a penny. Rolling in it. And lifted and laid too so they are. Well maybe not laid. Although you never know. That priest what-do-you-call-him, Father Cullinan, or Callanan is it, never did get his name right, that wears the leather jacket and bronze bracelet and lands in at dances in the parish hall smiling all round him, hail fellow well met, chatting to the girls, casual crafty hand round the back when he's leaving them, taking in all the close dancing that's going on and him laughing and chatting letting on not to be looking, hard to believe he's celibate. I'd say at the very least the same boy plays with his toys at night. And why wouldn't he, says you.

I just can't take it, that's what's wrong with me. Ham and eggs every morning they get (one sausage or two, Father?) and then around about half twelve they tuck into a nice lunch and they all finish up with a big feed of meat in the evening. Except Friday of course. Friday the day of abstinence, no haunch of venison or roast swan on Fridays, no, rules is rules, so they have to make do with wild salmon and *beurre blanc* sauce, cream potatoes, cauliflower, fresh carrots and garden peas.

Though they don't always get their own way. I heard a story Margaret the housekeeper over there told somebody. She comes into the dining-room one morning and Father Finucane's sitting at the breakfast table reading his mail and she's got the egg boiled and all and she says to him *You'll have a boiled egg Father?* And he says *No, I think I'll have a fry Margaret. Some bacon and egg and could you make it two sausages please?* And she says back to him *You'll have a fucking boiled egg Father.* And he says, nearly choking with the laughing, *I'll have a boiled egg Margaret.*

But that crowd at the wake couldn't have been more right about Maud and the money. You wouldn't have believed it to look at the cut of her and the shape of her house. Well she's booked her place in heaven now anyway. Come into the garden Maud, for the black bat Life has flown. Welcome to Paradise Maud, I am here at the gate alone; and the woodbine spices are wafted abroad and the musk of the rose is blown. Come sit on My right hand, O good and faithful servant, for your name is written in the book of heaven. No, hold on, on second thoughts, why don't you try this nice wee garden stool instead? No shortage of tulips here, what? See those blue ones over there? Especially for you. Don't mention it. Now, where was I? Ah yes, the book of heaven. Let's have a looky.

Hmm, you have indeed given sterling service to the church, to the tune of, let Me see, seven hundred and fifty thousand plus ninety-five thousand which, if I'm correct, comes to eight hundred and forty-five thou. Sweet music, Maud, sweet music down from the blissful skies indeed.

And We're not finished yet, are We? There

are also, ah, I've lost the place, yes, here We are, four houses, twenty-seven and three quarter acres of prime land plus the rest Maud, plus the rest. And the vintage Bentley of course, offside mudguard slightly rusted but no matter, that should fetch a fine penny. Now We'll overlook the Child of Prague who's missing two fingers and part of a nose anyway and the ducks and other wall furnishings which are pretty near worthless unless they're of sentimental value to somebody though I can't imagine. In fact you showed extremely good judgement there if I may say so, Maud. Pity about those neighbours of yours but in time they will learn to offer it up.

 I doubt it somehow. Maybe Mammy will but not me. She's only the executor. I'm the one has to do everything. In loco parentis. Loco's right. The second time at the probate office I was ready to kill somebody. Mammy's here to execute the will and I'm here to execute you you and you. You there sitting in your pinstriped three piece on your swivel chair with your nose in the air, prick, if you tell us we have to come back a third time I'm going to strangle you with this dental floss I have here with me in my pocket. Look, see it? And you too, Bob Cratchit, head down in your dusty ledger hiding behind your big desk trying to let on you don't see me. And I'll have more than enough left for you on my way out. Yes, you, you in your tacky uniform, what are you anyway but a fucking doorman? Two-bit job and you've the nerve to look at me like that.

+++++

To hell with them anyway. I can just hear them now, all those religious for want of a better word, smug as hell in their holy houses, lapping up their good fortune. But they can't take it with them can they? To hell with them, I've other things to think about. Would you believe I went to the Armagh march just to see her, not talk to her if she didn't want to talk, just see her, that would have been enough.

It's weird when you think about it, she lives a hundred yards away and I travel eighty or ninety miles just to try and get a look at her. And she was there, she was there. In the middle of thousands of civil rights marchers there she was, so close I could nearly have touched her. Ten thousand there must have been, singing We Shall Overcome, blocked by a Protestant counter-demonstration.

I saw her and she saw me. I had hardly time to take her in when she looked away to speak to a girl she was holding hands with. Audrey, it had to be Audrey, turned to look at me and it was then I got the shock. There was hardly anything of her but what there was was beautiful. The way I'd pictured her she was dowdy and plain and definitely butch. This girl was thin as a reed with nut-brown hair cropped short like a boy's but the furthest thing from a boy you could get.

The short hair showed off her full face and what a face it was, pale, near enough perfect as far as I could see, something classical about it, like a painting. My mind tried to remember as she fixed me with bright bold eyes. Virgin of the Rocks maybe. Only this was no virgin. The idea of these two beautiful girls doing whatever it was they did alone together was outlandish but there they were, lovers to each other. And they looked comfortable, defiant as they stood there hand in hand. Imagine if they could marry, imagine if that could happen, would

Aisling be the man? Who would wear the wedding dress? In my confusion I averted my gaze from Audrey to somewhere unfocused and when I looked back after I'm not sure how long she was still staring at me. What was that look? Curiosity, I'm sure of that, for she was seeing the man she had shared Aisling with, but there was something else. Looking at it now I think maybe it was guilt. Still holding hands they moved away and out of sight. Aisling. I'd hardly looked at her yet this was the girl that had transformed my life for a while, forever, and given me things no amount of sleep could dream.

  Maybe she's not there. I haven't called. Why? Why haven't I called? I don't even know. Maybe I'm afraid of what she might say. Of what I might say. I haven't seen her once here in Derry since the wake, not once, not in the street, not in her playschool, not in the City Hotel. Maybe she's moved, maybe she's gone up to Belfast to live with Audrey for good. That would nearly be a relief. Because then I'd know she was a lost cause and I could get on with things. Couldn't I?

+++++

For weeks now I've been walking the streets whispering her name and seeing her face in crowds everywhere I go. But she comes to me late at night always after I go to bed and her face is flushed with this kind of an opal light and each time she comes she reaches out as if to touch me and then goes away again.

    The night after Armagh I couldn't sleep thinking about her and how she makes love. Up dark and early and the way I felt as I shuffled to the bathroom I didn't think I'd ever be able to sleep again. No breakfast, breakfast was the last thing in my head. I closed the front door quietly behind me, stumbled along our path and the three steps down to the street, legs numb one second, sore and heavy the next. I'm not exactly sure why but I knew she'd be there this time, there in the flat, round the corner, down the hill, as if it was ordained. I wasn't thinking very straight and I'd no idea what I was going to say but I kept telling myself how she'd know to look at me that I loved her. All of her, body, soul, mind, everything. Wouldn't she? But here's a thing. When you haven't slept and you're out in the street and the day has hardly started and there's nobody about you see things you never saw before, not properly anyway, like roofs of houses and the slates dark and glossy from the rain and how big the chimneys are, unbelievable, big as coal sheds some of them, and the pigeons walking about with their hands behind their backs jerking their heads up and down at these invisible particles on the ground and others in the December chill fluffing their feathers and burying their beaks in their breasts and you see what pecking order means when a seagull lands in the middle of them all, oh you see it then all right. There wasn't another being except a dog outside the chemists hunkered down relieving itself. My heart felt as if it was leaving me at the thought of her, at the thought of the sight of her and the smell of her. And then I heard voices through the open doors of the cathedral and saw the worshippers' cars parked nose to tail on the hill. Eight o'clock mass it must be and the voices quavering out into the air.

> *I'll sing a hymn to Mary,*
> *The mother of my God,*
> *The virgin of all virgins,*

Of David's royal blood.
O teach me, holy Mary,
A loving song to frame,
When wicked men blaspheme thee
I'll love and bless thy name.
O Lily of the Valley,
O Mystic Rose, what tree
Or flower, e'en the fairest,
Is half so fair as thee.

Voices like a lament. The happiest hymns always sound like a lament in there. It must be the organist, he must be a depressive. I turned the handle of her street door and it opened and the stairs were in front of me, only the stairs and the door of the flat between us. The music was discordant now, suddenly discordant, twisting in the air, clashing with something, clashing with music from somewhere else, clashing with music coming from above. I pushed the door shut on all the lamenting and stood still. The Flower Duet. I held my breath and listened. In French was it? For moments the noise of my heart got in the way of hearing but then I heard. Yes, in French, two sweet voices. I remembered it and what happened the very first time she played it in French.

> *Sous le dôme épais où le blanc jasmin*
> *A la rose s'assemble*
> *Sur la rive en fleurs riant au matin.*

Oh Jesus. I leaned on the banister light with the enchantment. I took the stairs in a rush then and stopped to hear again at the closed door, pictured her lying on the big wide bed listening to the music and thinking back to us together and in the middle of it remembering me yesterday just feet away, heart going out to me and wanting to come to me but afraid of the rebuff, lying now remembering us together.

The door fell open at my touch and I saw WORKERS UNITE AND FIGHT on a placard up against the sofa and smelt the incense and saw the candle burning on the low table by the unlit lamp. The flame bowed as I came in and then withdrew for a moment before righting itself. A girl's voice said Yes, yes, do it, please do it again! and I heard the dull thwack and a cry of pain and Aisling saying

There, that's enough. I'll put it away now. Are you all right? Here, let me look at you. Oh my poor love. Let me put this on you.

Put what on you? I stood at the locked street door. Discordant notes wavered in the wet air, lugubrious notes long drawn out from the wide-open cathedral doors. They're asleep in each other's arms up there or in Belfast, sleeping off a night of love. Here or in Belfast, what does it matter?

I hurried home under a lowering sky and bent my head against the rain. Outside the chemist's I slipped on something and fell hard on one knee, rose, turned into Marlborough Terrace, limped, smelt the shit, limped and felt no pain.

They were singing another hymn to Mary now and their voices followed me from the cathedral to the house and they didn't stop till I slammed the front door.

> *O Mother I could weep for mirth*
> *Joy fills my heart so fast.*
> *My soul today is heaven on earth—*
> *O would this transport last.*

"Would you look at you, you're wringing," Mammy said. "What were you doing out there anyway without a coat? And what are you looking at me like that for? What did *I* do?"

+++++

I'm in the City Hotel five nights a week now. Turning into a bit of a habitual drinker. But sometime she'll come. She has to surely, she has so many friends in Derry that she'll want to come back to see, she'll have to come. And until she does there's always company, no shortage of company. Doesn't fill the void, but still. Marxist suicide marchers, other left-wing allsorts, Nationalist party stalwarts, Citizens' Action Committee celebrities, spongers, sex-seekers. Sometime she'll come.

Thursdays and Fridays I sit at home with Mammy and look at TV. A man could grow old this way. On Friday we watch *The Late Late Show*. Stupid name of course because it's not late late, it's not even late. It starts at half nine and ends at eleven or so when the night's only starting. Anyway, I was sitting watching it with Mammy this time and they were discussing the pope's encyclical about birth control and of course the Pill had to be brought into the conversation. There was a theologian on about the spiritual dangers of using it and then a lady doctor started explaining how it can harm a woman's health or maybe even kill her.

Mammy always switches over if there's anything to do with sex on but this time she turned the volume up. You wanted to hear it. Breast cancer, cervical cancer, blood clots, gall bladder disease, liver tumours, bad cholesterol, infertility, genital warts and all these other sexually transmitted diseases, everything but ingrown toenails and maybe those too if she'd had the time to get round to them.

Mammy was nodding away at her head the whole way through it and I sat thinking, Typical!—that's Telefís Éireann all over, just giving one side of the story. Now this boy Gay Byrne's the presenter and he made a bit of an effort to act as devil's advocate but you'd have thought by the end of it he was the devil himself the way some people in the audience were going on. He was lucky he didn't end up tarred and feathered.

Then as a bit of relief they brought on these

Irish dancers. It's a funny thing about Irish dancing. There they were, the girls high-stepping and you could see their legs right up to their panties and beyond if you looked hard enough and their hands were dead stiff by their sides and the boys dancing next to them weren't going near them and they had their hands down the same way. There may as well have been a sign up saying Don't touch, this is Ireland, this is Irish culture, don't go on the way depraved ones do with their jiving and slow dancing and miniskirts. It's no wonder most of the country's screwed up. Short shrift to short shifts. Priestridden Ireland. No, that doesn't sound right.

It was supposed to be one of my drink-free nights but I thought, What a ridiculous country and I told Mammy I was going out for a walk. She said something, sounded like she wasn't happy about me going out for a walk on one of my nights in, but I wasn't listening.

I headed down Creggan Hill levitating for the length it took me to pass Aisling's flat. A quiver in the waterworks. I paused at the top of William Street and peered through the dark. Stopped breathing for a bit and listened for the sounds of rioting. Things seemed quiet as I walked on but you can never be sure in this town. Like a graveyard one minute and the next it's carnival time. Friendly nod from two guys leaning up against the Grandstand bar looking to tap me for the price of a drink maybe. That was a good one Mickey MacTamm told me the last time he was cutting my hair.

As God's me witness I seen it happening meself Jeremiah. His Lordship the bishop walking down William Street last Saturday. I see you shaking your head there but I'm telling you now, he was walking all right. On his own too, I swear it. Naw listen, sure didn't I see him with me own eyes? I was coming up the ways on the other side of the street and I nearly dropped so I did. Never seen that man walking in me life before, always in the back of the big Rolls any time I seen him. Wait, I tell a lie. I seen him one time walking up the middle aisle in the cathedral there around Corpus Christi I think it was and a whole gang of men holding the canopy thing over him. Is that what you call it? You know the thing I'm talking about, like the roof of a circus tent if you can picture it.

Well he's going down past the Grandstand twirling away at the big black umburella and these three standing outside arguing the odds for the day look up and there he is. So all together they salute him and then they say one after the other Good morning your lordship and you know what he does? He looks up at the Guildhall clock and sees it's two minutes past twelve so he says back to them Good afternoon and walks on, head in the air. Put them in their place so he did.

William Street quiet, still strewn with bricks and stones from the day's rioting, but quiet for now. Turned into Waterloo Place, passed couples walking hand in hand, others in doorways grinding up against one another, up for anything I'd say, making me remember, filling my throat, stopping me breathing nearly, soon to be stretched some of them on sofas, car back seats, beds, glutinous seed emptying, filling, infecting.

A police car hurtled through Guildhall Square, cop in the back seat gave me the fingers. Or maybe it was the V sign. Amounts to the same thing. She might be there. That programme about lesbians I saw on TV last week, somewhere in the north of England. Newcastle was it? Doesn't matter where it was. Interesting. No, fascinating. No, titillating. Out of focus shots of bodies rolling and writhing in slow motion, pastel fluids running into each other, breasts merging. Mammy came into the kitchen in the middle of it and I was nearly going to change channels and then I thought, Why the hell should I? I pay the bloody rental. She didn't catch on till it was nearly over anyway, stupid you see, when this dyke said I prefer girls meself, men are hard see and adding My mar knows nowt aboot it. Well she knows now, dear, she knows now. My mar wanted it switched off but I held out. She made a scene and I couldn't take in this part at the end properly with bottoms going up and down like billows, pale red and pink and purple, really arty and all, great camerawork but I couldn't appreciate it. Stuff her, I saw as much as I wanted to see anyway. Still feel disappointed it never talked about bisexual girls though. Probably there's so few they'd have to trawl for ages to find ones.

  Hardly in the door of the City Hotel when I saw her. Her. Disappearing round the corner into the bar. Didn't see me. Hair different, cut short, dyed some kind of brown, first thing I noticed. Urchin look like Mia Farrow, face pale, what was it she was in? *Rosemary's Baby*. Like Audrey. Exactly like Audrey. Tight black shiny. Jesus, it's leather, that's leather she's wearing, two piece leather suit. Who's she with? Who's she with? I'll go in there in a minute, go to the men's first to think. How long ago was it she told me she wasn't sleeping? She looks great. She looks fantastic. She looks happy. How can she be happy?

The man talking to the receptionist was unmistakable. Grey broad-brimmed hat, Zapata moustache. Big Vinny Coyle, chief civil rights steward, salt of the earth, stopped me being crushed half to death that time at the Armagh march.

"Ah she's made it all right," he said. "She commands amazing fees now you know."

"I say she's past her best." Golden thickly lacquered crowning glory inclined towards him, adroitly he evaded with deft swerve of the head.

"Think so?" Vinny tilted the fedora back a bit. "I was reading there about her saying she wouldn't get out of her bed for less than five thousand."

Gurgle of laughter from the golden head nearly choking. "I wonder now how much she charges to get in."

Vinny raised an admonishing finger. "Now Majella. A Catholic girl like you shouldn't be coming out with them kinda things. That's calumny. Do you know what calumny is?"

"I do not."

"Do you not remember from your catechism? It means taking away a person's good name, that's what it means. And a Catholic girl like you..."

"I never knew she had a good name."

Vinny turned his eyes to heaven and his head away and that's when he saw me standing there rooted. "Ah hello Master Coffey. How you doing? Is the rain staying off out there?"

I moved my feet and went towards him. Who's she with?

"Aye, it's still dry. How you doing anyway? I never got thanking you right for what you did up in Armagh Vinny."

Vinny blinked kindly. "Not at all Master. I trust you were okay after that? You were being sort of roughed up by our own side. What's this they say? With friends like that? Did you see Aisling?"

"Who?"

"Aisling O'Connor."

"I did. She was just across the road from us."

"Naw, I mean, did you not see her in here? She just got back the day. Wasn't it terrible about that friend of hers?"

"Who?"

"That girl she was great with from Belfast. Did you not hear?"

"What?"

"She was killed in an accident up there when was it? It was just after the Armagh march I think, the day after or maybe two days. Did you not hear? I thought you'd have heard. Wall fell on her in the big storm, remember the big storm? Somewhere up the Whiterock Road as far as I know. Terrible thing. I thought you'd have heard seeing—"

"Would that have been? What girl?"

He half closed his eyes and directed his gaze above and beyond me, his lips moving slowly as he went over names in his head. The hotel lobby turned noisy suddenly as a crowd of people came rushing in the front door.

"Audrey I think her name was." He was nearly shouting above the noise. "I can't mind her last name but her and Aisling were very close. Real socialist so she was. She was one of the first ones to join the People's Democracy you know. Big loss, she's a big loss. Are you all right Master? Here, sit down. Look, there's a chair there."

He touched my elbow and ushered me towards an armchair near the door. "Do you not want to sit down? Why do they let in them sort of people anyway? You'd think they'd have somebody on the door so you would. Here, sit there a minute. Tell me this now. Do you ever get headaches after what happened on the fifth?"

"Fifth?"

"October. Fifth of October. Hospitality of the RUC. Do you get headaches do you?"

"Naw, I'm over that. Listen, thanks Vinny. I'm all right. I just got a bit of a shock. I didn't know a thing about it. I think I'll go into the bar for a while."

"Aisling'll be there. You'll see her in there. Look out for that man teaches in your school though. Master O'Reilly."

"Pearse? How do you mean?"

"I'd stay clear of him if I were you. He's going to get himself thrown out the way he's going on."

"Sure Pearse is off the drink. He's been off it since …" I couldn't remember. She was there.

"Well he's not off it tonight. He's shooting off his mouth at everybody he meets."

I didn't see her at first. But I saw Pearse sitting with Michael Cole and I could tell right away he was off the wagon. He had a whiskey glass in his hand and there was something about the loose way he was holding it that told me it was far from his first that night. But after those few seconds it hardly fizzed on me, just this feeling of dull disappointment that was away in no time. I gave the two of them a vague nod and Michael nodded back and smiled but Pearse didn't notice me. Then I saw her. She was at a table to the side of them with some girl I never saw before. I went and held out my hand and my fingers were trembling.

"Vinny Coyle was just telling me there about Audrey. I'm sorry Aisling. That was such a terrible thing to happen."

It wasn't anything like my voice I was hearing. She took my hand in hers. I wasn't sorry. Was she? She held my hand tentatively and the softness and the warmth suffused me. The street was grey the last time I saw her, the night we waked Maud, the night the children's swings in Bull Park got swallowed in the dew.

"Thanks Jeremiah." She held onto my hand as I was taking it away. Just for that extra part of a second. Old time's sake? Her eyes were on me, turquoise gleam, I tried to read them and couldn't, waited for more, anything, an introduction to the one beside her even. Who was the one beside her? Bit of a welterweight, looked like a dyke to be honest, square-looking face the colour of white chalk, eyes I couldn't see, black polo neck, dark hair cut short like the military get done, more man than woman, made me think of some of these ones I saw on the marches, dressed like men some of them, feminists denying their femininity, this way of looking at you meant to make you shrivel.

Was she Aisling's comfort now in these mourning days and nights? No introduction. What did that tell? I stood on, five seconds, ten, I don't know, and then I began to turn away and saw her lips parting, lips that kissed me everywhere, remembered her voice hoarse with wanting every time she saw me again.

"I'll see you anyway," she said. I saw my fingers detach themselves from the rest of me and reach out to the loose little bow at the neck. The whole thing slid down her shimmering back and was held for a moment, sweet moment, at the swell of her thighs until with barely a twitch she made it fall the rest of the way to the floor leaving her bottom and its bone-white furrow bare. "Now strap me up," she whispered.

"The last tortoise I had," Michael said. "Wee bugger. Honest to Christ you couldn't take your eyes off him any length of time. You'd sit there watching him for ages and he wouldn't move a muscle but do you see if you turned your back for one second, he was away on you and you never saw him again. I don't know how many tortoises I lost that way."

"Fuck off," said Pearse.

"I'll see you anyway."

That's what she said. I'll see you anyway. She wants to see me again. I sat down beside Michael and Pearse, legs not there, rest of me light as a summer cloud.

"How's tricks?"

"Not bad Michael. And you?"

"Not so good. Got shot down at the dance there and drowning my sorrows."

"Droning your sorrows you mean," said Pearse.

"Hey, Pearse is fierce hard on me tonight, no sympathy at all."

"Why don't you just fuck off Cole."

Michael gave him a look then and put the glass to his mouth and swallowed the last of his drink in a rush.

"Must go. Best of luck anyway."

He was still within earshot when Pearse said to me: "Eejit so he is. Empty-headed tithead."

"I was thinking of going myself. Are you heading?" I'd go and then come back when I got shot of him.

"What are you on about? I'm only here twenty minutes. Why would I be heading?"

"Naw, I was just thinking—"

"I was in Tracy's there and some muscle-bound thug on the door turfed me out and all I was doing was talking a bit of politics with this arsehole in a tweed jacket. Tweed fucking jacket. What would you say about a man wears a tweed jacket?"

"I don't know. Maybe talking politics isn't the best thing to do when you've drink in you."

"What the fuck you talking about? Sure that's all they do in this place here. Religion and politics. I'm getting out to fuck to Manchester anyway. Did you know this? Did you ever know this? The absent presence of God's supposed to be the thing keeps the churches going and it's nothing but an absence of course, all it is is a pretence of a presence that isn't there at all. The whole thing's a political smokescreen with vestments on. And the politics they talk here in this bloody town isn't so much politics as shite. And you'd think to listen to them they were over on the left bank of the Seine. Some of this crowd think they're real bohemians, you know that? See them two over there?"

"Who?"

"Right behind you, them two you were talking to a minute ago."

He turned his head to look at Aisling's table and all astir I followed his gaze. The black leather was tight on her breasts and shoulders. She was in rapt conversation with her friend and her face was so pale and her eyes were bigger and bluer than I'd ever seen them. Why was that? Was it the short hair did it, made her eyes look that way, gave her the waif look? Maybe she wasn't eating.

"Listen to them, they're still at it. I could hear them every time Cole drew breath. They're all for justice and they wouldn't know what it was if it hit them up the fanny. Say nothing, just listen to them."

I said nothing and listened. I listened to her voice and tasted her again.

"I always thought it was a work in progress but Audrey kept saying it was a betrayal of socialist principles."

"See what I mean? Shite."

"Shh. They'll hear you."

"It was just the way we were treated

differently from the permanent ones, you know, the kibbutzniks. They'd all these privileges. But Rome wasn't built in a day. I tried to tell—"

"Aye," said Pearse swinging round to glare at her, had more than enough of it from the look of him, "and it'll take a few more days for the bastards to wipe out the rest of the Palestinians so it will."

Aisling turned her head in our direction. I lowered my eyes.

"Sorry, were you talking to me?" she asked. She was shaken but she wasn't going to let it pass.

"Naw," said Pearse, "I was talking about you."

"Oh?"

"Aye, oh deary me. I couldn't help hearing your sanctimonious claptrap. You and this Audrina one that were in the kibbutz splitting hairs over the rights yous were given, out there following the fashion with your phoney do-gooding. Social equality, isn't that what the thing's supposed to be about? What the hell were yous doing in that bloody commune when the ones that worked their land in Palestine for hundreds of years have no equality at all? How would you like your olive groves that have been there for yonks cut down every turnabout? How would you like your house knocked down and your land and water taken off you? How in under fuck can you sit out there in a fucking kibbutz that's supposed to be about Marxist principles when the Palestinians are treated like shite? I never heard anything so fucking ridiculous in my life."

Aisling's eyes flashed. "Who do you think you are to be making judgements—"

"I'm someone can see the wood for the trees, that's who."

"Have you ever been there?" she demanded.

"Don't have to go. Would I want to go to South Africa when I know what the whites are doing to the blacks? Naw, and I wouldn't want to go to your precious Israel either. Listen missy, can you name me another country that's not an island that hasn't got a border?"

Aisling stared at him, mouth open, beautiful, bemused. "And you know why they've no border between them and the Palestinians?" he said half shouting. "Because there's no limit to what they intend to take. Like all the land they stole in the six day war they organised. Sure their whole bloody rule comes from grubby deals." He was holding his glass so tight you'd have thought it was going to break. "Tell us this and tell us no more. How many Palestinians did you see working in that kibbutz? How many?"

Her face was even paler now and she looked as if she was raring to go the second he took a breath which he didn't look as if he was going to do. "You know why you saw none? Cause the Israelis wouldn't have one about the place. Like who was it, what do you call him, Brookeborough, the last prime minister in this place before O'Neill, that's what Brookeborough said about us. I wouldn't have one about the place."

"It's not the same kind of thing!" These words from the dyke. Funny voice, squeaky wee voice, like a boy's voice breaking, not what you'd have expected to look at her. Big ugly Adam's apple on her, up and down as she spoke. Could be a man trapped in a woman's body. I've heard of that, genitals tucked away inside.

Pearse turned his head sharply to take her in. "Aw aye it is, dear, it's exactly the same kind of thing. It's the same as the Brits did here with their penal laws and their plantations. I'd say from the look of the two of you you're out marching for Catholic rights. Am I right? Am I?"

The last two words were so loud some heads turned.

"Take it easy Pearse," I said laying my hand on his arm. "Keep your voice down."

He pulled his arm violently away. "What the fuck are you talking about? What the fuck has it got to do with you?"

"I happen to know one of them and there's no call for you—"

"We're not out for Catholic rights. We're not sectarian. How dare you!"

This was Aisling. There was a haze around her. Maybe it was my eyes that did it but there was a haze around her. The thought of her touch settled on my heart. We lay together embraced laughing the morning after the night I took her to casualty, the morning she rang the school pretending to be Mammy.

"Crowd of crooked landgrabbers, racist government, and yous can't even see. Typical City Hotel socialists sipping your vodka and whites. Take your hand away from me Jerry boy. You can go and fuck the two of them if that's what you want. As long as you know they can't see past their noses."

I hadn't realised I was holding his arm again. He stood up and my hand fell away. "Best of luck citizens," he said picking up his glass and emptying what was in it down his throat. He knocked against me as he went to go and then he was away, weaving between the tables.

"I'm sorry about that," I said.

"Is he a friend of yours?" said squareface.

"Well he works with me. He'd given up the drink but he's obviously back on it again."

"Obviously," said squareface needlessly, implying by her tone that I was some kind of accessory.

"He's a good fella when he's sober but he was way out of order there. I'm sorry he insulted you."

"Why should you be sorry?" Aisling pointed

out. "It wasn't your fault." Paused. "Why don't you sit here."

Mutely I did just that, lifting my chair over and putting it down beside Aisling and away from her companion. Mutely because I was trembling and didn't trust myself to speak. The dyke didn't look too pleased.

"When did you hear about Audrey?" Aisling said hoarsely.

I swallowed, coughed and swallowed again. "Just tonight there. Vinny told me when I came in. What an awful thing to happen."

"She was taking a group of children up for some activities in Saint Thomas's school in the Whiterock when a wall started to collapse. She pushed them out of the way and those two seconds were what ..."

She tailed off and put her hand to her forehead. When she was ready to speak again she said: "She was the most generous person I ever met. Oh sorry, this is Frances, this is Jeremiah." Frances with an e or Francis with an i? Our eyes met, gooseberries eyeballing each other.

"What will you have to drink?" I asked. "Aisling? Frances?"

Aisling waved a hand over her glass shaking her head and her friend seeing this did the same.

"We were actually thinking of going," Aisling said. "We just came in for the one." She started to get up. Her black leather skirt rose from behind the table, tight, pleated, hugging her. Frances stood and so did I. Body all aglow now I said: "I was just about to go myself. Sure I'll walk up with yous."

+++++

Everything quiet on the William Street front. Somebody was singing round a corner somewhere as we negotiated the scattered bricks and stones. Yellow Submarine. He could sing whoever it was. Better than the Beatle that sang it anyway, the drummer was it? Ringo Starr. Others joined in each time he came back to the chorus but they weren't so good.

"You wouldn't think there was a revolution going on," said Aisling. Her shoulder kept touching mine as I walked between the two of them.

"I heard it was like that in Paris," Frances said. She moved heavy in the black Crombie that covered her shapelessness. There's money there. Unless of course she got it from some penitent capitalist via the Saint Vincent de Paul. "People would be sitting eating and drinking at tables outside restaurants and round the corner it was all happening." She really had an unfortunate voice, falsetto nearly, expressionless, awful. The sound of her would have annoyed me even if I hadn't thought she'd been lying with Aisling. "Margarita was telling me that time she came back. Margarita was there for the whole thing you know."

I felt a tingle every time her shoulder touched mine. Halos round the lights of the lampposts, frost in the air everywhere, excitement pulling at me. Funny thing about the sky that night, you could still see stars even with all the lights. I was looking up as the dyke was talking, trying to fix my mind on something else, and there was this particular star above the trees in the cathedral grounds that kept winking away. Stellar something they call that. It was on The Sky at Night but I can never take in half of what Patrick Moore is saying because his face distracts me. He's talking about gases in the atmosphere and stuff and I'm trying to understand but I'm looking at him staring at me with one mad eye and the hair everywhere. Stellar constellation, that was it. To do with turbulence and I don't know what else. The nearness of what could happen quickened my heart. And above the trees the spire pointed skywards, reminding, sentineled over the city.

"Watch yourself," said Aisling and gripped my arm. Christ that was a near one. Bloody bricks.

"You could break your ankle here if you're not careful," she said and held my arm the rest of the way up to her flat. Above the trees the steeple pierced the blackness pointing skywards. My heart quickened, soaring.

"She was arrested," explained Frances, "and when the judge asked her name she said Rudi Dutschke, you know the German student leader that was shot, and he says That, miss, is a man's name. What is your real name please? And she says Janek Litynski and the judge thought she said Janet and so did the clerk of the court and the clerk wrote it down."

"Jan Litynski that led the Polish revolution there in January?" Aisling was laughing. "They never heard of him?"

"Never heard of him," said Frances.

Did you ever feel you couldn't relate to what people were talking about? You could understand what they were saying but you couldn't relate to it? Well the way they started going on then Aisling and your woman obviously felt they'd some kind of kinship with these ones in Berlin and Paris and Warsaw is it, whatever the capital of Poland is. Not that I cared mind you, I was too busy trying to keep my heart in order. But I remember now it was Pearse went on to me one time about how the situations in these places weren't like each other at all and weren't like here either. Difference of night and day, he said, these doctrinarians are making an artificial connection. Why would they do that? I asked him. Because they're wankers, he said. On the other hand, if you listened to Eamonn McCann you'd start to wonder, although the same guy could probably convince a lecture hall of academics that the nineteen forty phone directory for Dublin was the first draft of James Joyce's unfinished masterpiece. I heard him one night in the Gweedore Bar coming out with some weird stuff, weird but plausible that is, everything McCann says sounds plausible, about six degrees of separation and this middle eastern philosopher boy called Oz Moses. At least that's what I thought he was saying and it was only when I said to Pearse What do you reckon about Oz Moses? and he said Osmosis? Yeah, interesting concept, that I caught on it wasn't a man at all.

Pearse knows a lot, probably he knows too much and that's what's wrong with him, too much knowledge being a dangerous thing as I heard a Redemptorist priest saying one time he came to give a retreat in the cathedral. Osmosis is supposed to be, he said, Pearse that is, about picking up information without realising you're doing it but there's a whole lot of hooey talked about it too of course, like you and the world combining and crap like that.

"Would you like to come in awhile?"

We'd got to outside her flat and we were standing there looking at each other and Frances must have felt a bit out of it. We were looking at each other and I couldn't read her face because it was in shadow but I'd say she could read mine with the light of the lamppost behind her shining right on me. I don't know what my expression was but whatever it was I would have gone up those stairs on my knees if she'd asked me to.

"May as well," I said.

The first thing I saw when I closed the door of the flat was Kitty Birch right in my face swinging on the hook. Kitty Birch, instrument of divine torture. Spanking new, Aisling told me laughing the first time she showed it to me. And still framed on the wall outside the bedroom door were me and the Royal Ulster Constabulary with their blurred batons over my head, frozen at ten past four, fifth of October, and me still hanging onto the no waiting sign.

"Sit down there and I'll get yous something. Let me see. I only have whiskey. Hold on, there's a bit of Bacardi left. And I think there's Coke in the fridge. What do you say?" She looked at me first. "A drop of whiskey would be great," I said. No harm loosening up. Only the one though. Any more and.

"I'll have a rum and Coke thanks," Frances said.

Her squeaky voice was really getting to me.

Everything about her was off-key, hair sticking up now like a squaddie in shock, face so pale you'd have thought she dipped it in a bag of flour, like gothic or something, shoulders up to her ears, eyes away back in her head, shapeless black jeans to go with the black polo she kept pulling up over her chin. That would be anxiety. Her night's plans disrupted. I knew from the set of her face she could have seen me far but at the back of it all she was probably settling for three in the bed.

Aisling was stooped getting Coke from the fridge. "I see you still have the photo on the wall," I said, heart going like mad. The pleated leather skirt had come up a fair bit showing most of the back of her legs as she bent and when she turned she caught me looking and blushed. "If I was a believer," she said smoothing her skirt, "I'm sure I'd have Saint Antony or somebody like that up there but seeing I'm not ..."

"I was talking to a cop the other day," I told her, "down at Kevin McLaughlin's. You know, the car dealer down the Buncrana Road."

"Right?" said Aisling. She handed us the drinks and sat beside the table-lamp which she then lighted. Her face had got thinner, I could see that now, and it wasn't just the urchin hair that did it. And very pale. Ruby lipstick she had on brought out the paleness.

"Aye, friendly guy and all."

"Why, does that surprise you?" said Frances. "That he was friendly?" She was challenging me. Looking back on it now it wasn't surprising. I was a man and a rival to boot and she'd probably made up her mind that I was an outsider of the left-wing loony club. I blinked at her with this perplexed look on my face trying to make her feel foolish. I might as well have been blinking at Lenin's statue. "I'm not sure what you mean," I said.

"You sounded as if you had them stereotyped, that's all."

"Stereotyped?" Fuck her. I'd rather be doubly incontinent than heaving up against this one. "I don't know where you got that idea from."

"That friend of yours down in the hotel. I gathered you were bosom buddies the way you were defending him. Well, birds of a—"

"I wasn't exactly defending him dear. I was explaining him."

Her eyes flashed at the dear and Aisling intervened.

"Hey you two, take it easy. What were you saying Jeremiah? God it's cold, isn't it? I'm just feeling it now so I am." She rose quickly and clicked the superser twice and then sat down again. The blue and yellow flame appeared, flickered and steadied. "Sorry, what were you saying?"

"Naw it was just that I changed to a Beetle recently and—"

"Oh I didn't know you'd changed. What's it like?"

"Great except when you're turning a corner it's like driving a ten ton lorry."

"I heard that about them. But they're very dependable aren't they?"

"I dunno yet. I haven't had it long enough yet to know."

"But you were saying anyway."

"Aye. This fella was asking me how I was managing with it and I told him I'd a problem getting used to the dip switch on the floor. You know the way in other cars you've got it up beside the steering. Anyway he started advising me about the dip because he had a Beetle himself and then he said I'm a policeman, maybe you won't want to be talking to me when you hear that. I was sort of caught unawares and I said Not at all. I was thinking afterwards he could have been one of those guys up there on the wall."

Aisling laughed. That tinkle again. The waves of heat quivered in the cold air and the faint smell of gas brought back our first time, the night of the fifth.

"Do you see what I was saying there about Margarita and all?" piped up the dyke, effortlessly changing the subject. "I don't care what anybody says, there's an energy in these things, it's like a force, why else would all these movements be happening at the one time?"

So much for me and the friendly cop. This was weighty stuff.

"I agree," said Aisling. "I think it's going to be unstoppable. It's like what Marx and Rosa Luxemburg dreamed of. What's this it was she said? The socialist proletariat are going to be the gravediggers of world capitalism?"

"That's exactly right," said Frances, blockhead

up and down like a piston. "The socialist proletariat are going to be the gravediggers of world capitalism. Things that are fights for survival at the start turn into revolutions. And they all become connected. They intersect, that's the thing."

What are they anyway? Do they ever listen to themselves? My eyes fell for a moment on the worn carpet where she'd stood wet from the shower and the pink halter neck plastered to her skin. She'd shaken with laughter against me and I'd felt her damp in my shirt and trousers.

"Frances is doing a doctorate on Roger Casement you know," she said.

That figures. That's the boy got young black men to bugger him night and day.

"Right enough?" I said. "I did a bit on him."

"Where was that?" asked Frances without interest.

"Ah, A-level history. And I've read newspaper articles about him since. Very interesting man."

"A-level history?" Same deadpan squeak.

"That's right."

"Well this is an in depth study. It's going to take me three years. I've just finished my Masters."

Bully for you bitch.

"Frances knows just about everything there is to know about Casement," said Aisling.

"That's brilliant," I lied. "What was it attracted you to him?"

"His evolution I suppose. And no matter what he did he put his heart and soul into it. You know about his time in the Congo don't you? I expect you covered that."

Not everything. Not the messy details.

"You probably remember that Leopold of Belgium turned the Congo into his own private colony and called it the Congo Free State. Well it was a million times less free than even the so-called Free State we have over the border here. It was a massive labour camp and I'm sure you know he murdered millions of people just so he could get a fortune out of the rubber and copper there. Do you remember learning that? His mercenaries burned thousands of villages and every single time they did that they trussed up the women spread-eagled in such a way they could be conveniently raped."

I nodded mechanically as if all this was old

hat. Was that relish in her voice? Yes it was. She rubbed her mouth with the back of her hand. Not a pleasant sight but out of the corner of my eye I knew that Aisling was gazing steadfastly at her. Admiringly? I didn't want to look.

"They made the village men watch the raping going on and then they told them it wouldn't stop till the men went into the jungle and brought back so many hundredweight of rubber from the wild vines. It seems this was a terrible painful thing to do and took forever. And usually of course they weren't able to bring enough back and that meant they all got their throats cut, women as well as men. The children were forced to sit and watch all this and then they got the same. Throats cut," she added helpfully.

"That's awful," Aisling said.

Frances was pleased with the impact. She smiled hungrily at Aisling, mouth gaping smiling but no smile in her eyes that I could see, hidden eyes hiding her thoughts. I thought how strange the human mind that someone of Aisling's beauty and refinement could allow herself to be pawed by this monstrosity. Ones like her used to go away and stay locked in convents but there's more of them at large now, more and more of them every time you turn round. Can't get a man for love or money so they make friendships with lonely girls and before you know it.

"Anyway," said Frances, "Casement was appointed by the British government to find out what was going on and his report put a stop to Leopold's Free State." She sighed a put on sigh. "If ever there was a misnomer that was it."

It was then the nerves got to me because I didn't think I could listen any longer to that freak whining out her data. "Casement's time in Africa turned him anti-British, right?" I blurted.

"Well it wasn't as simple as that," she said to Aisling. "There were stages. He was sort of crazy mixed-up when he was a teenager. He thought British rule should be everywhere no matter what it took but Charles Stewart Parnell was his hero at the same time. And you can't get much more crazy mixed-up than that. I'd say it was really the Boer war and the British concentration camps that changed him and of course straight after this he was sent to the Congo and that put the tin lid on it, he was an anti-imperialist from then on. What was it he wrote when the Brits sent him to South America?"

It wasn't really a question. From her tone you knew you were going to have to wait for that particular piece of information. Her eyelids closed while she remembered. Then it came. "I'm a queer sort of a British consul. I should really be in one of their jails instead of under the Lion and Unicorn."

"Sounds like the name of a pub," I said. Nerves again.

She stared at me, forehead furrowed with exaggerated irritation. "Do you know what the Lion and Unicorn are?"

"Well I used to drink in a place with a name very like that every payday the summer I worked in Forte's Coffee House in Piccadilly. It was round the corner in Leicester Square. Now I think of it that was the name and all. Nearly next to the Mitre bar where Charles Laughton used to drink."

"You don't know what they are, don't you not? They're symbols of the United Kingdom, the lion and the unicorn are symbols of the United Kingdom." She shook her head.

The bitch wasn't getting away with it. I'd tell her a thing or two she didn't know.

"Our history teacher reckoned Casement was unhinged," I said. Bingo, better effect than I could have hoped for. Black sockets widened till they seemed to take up about a quarter of her face, mouth open like a dead flounder. So far so good.

"Aye, I remember him saying he was a typical Protestant convert to the Irish Nationalist cause. How's this now he put it?"

I actually couldn't remember how he'd put it but that wasn't going to stop me.

"Full of guilt," I said, "for the way England treated Ireland and hadn't a clue how the ordinary Prod felt about all these uprisings."

She was speechless. I'd got her speechless. I was on a roll, no question.

"Do you know where he was captured?" I said this eyeing her steadily.

The dark pits were impassive but the mouth had started to move, still didn't speak though.

"I was actually there."

"Is that right?" encouraged Aisling nervously.

"Where?"

"The Centre Spot restaurant up in Letterkenny. I've eaten there. Casement was caught in it by British forces. It was actually Laird's Hotel then. He was sitting in French uniform having his breakfast and a guy that used to study law with him recognised him and informed." Stick that in your fucking pipe, dyke.

She didn't just stick it in her pipe, she smoked it furiously and then knocked the ashes out on top of my head while they were still hot. "Really? Did you say you studied this? You're about a hundred and twenty years and four hundred miles out friend. You're thinking of Wolfe Tone. Roger Casement was captured at McKenna's fort in Kerry. Christ."

Aisling to the rescue. "Time for a refill," she said and hurried to the worktop. "Here, give us your glass there," and came over to me, hand outstretched, not taking no for an answer kind of way.

"Thanks Aisling. A tiny taste will do me." I hadn't intended taking any more but being a little shaken just then I didn't argue.

She took my glass to where the bottle was and poured in far too much. "Oops. Sorry about that Jeremiah. I'm sure you won't complain though." She gave me the drink, eyes lingering, fingers lingering, fingers closing over my knuckles.

"Frances?" she said turning part of the way round to her friend sitting there with a face of stone on her, I'd say because Aisling's hand was still on mine, absentmindedly like.

"I think I'll go to my bed" was the answer she got and with that the black mass began to haul itself out of the armchair.

My bed. *Her* bed. There was only one bed in the flat and that was through the door to my right.

"Stay where you are sure," said Aisling quickly. "What's your hurry anyway? Here, take a wee Bacardi." And she took her hand from mine and went and pushed Frances playfully back. Relenting at the touch the gargoyle subsided.

"All right then, just the one more," she said.

Drinks served, Aisling went back beside the lamp. I knew she was looking for something safe to say, something light that wouldn't raise hackles. Not an easy thing to do because trivialities that keep the rest of us going half the time seemed to have no place on this bitch's agenda, not even under any other business. The silence was long and getting longer when Aisling broke it.

"I don't know how I'm going to go on the People's Democracy march with Audrey not there," she said. She put her hand quickly to her forehead. More than the ruby lipstick it was the light from the lamp now I think that made her paler even than she was. And made her dyed hair look flaxen too, like one of those Dutch girls Vermeer painted. Girl with a Pearl Earring, that was the one I'm nearly sure. The sultry wench who posed for as long as he needed. Except it was those big hoops Aisling had on, whatever they call them, like tarnished silver circles coming down nearly to her shoulders. Only ever saw her in earrings once before and she was beautiful in them, the night, yes, the night she had her hair up and I took it down and she let me undress her.

"Why, are you going to be marching again?" I asked.

"Did you not know? Sure it's in the papers." She picked up a newspaper from the floor, folded it and tossed it to me. "It's on the front there."

I scanned the front page. STUDENT MARCHERS PLAN TO CUT A SWATHE THROUGH ULSTER–PAISLEY. People's Democracy activists are intending holding a four-day march across Northern Ireland starting from Belfast on the first of January and ending in Derry on the fourth.

"Taking John Bull by the horns?" I said. She'd be wanting me to go on it. I'd go. I handed the paper back to her.

Aisling smiled, tears shining. "You could say that. I think we've had enough of the half loaves our beloved prime minister's been handing out and the way the media's treating him like some kind of hero. This thing's going to die the death if we don't do something."

"We can't be naive about this," added Frances. "Paisley's right in a way for once. We know we're going to provoke. We're going to be marching through Protestant areas that Catholics never marched before. Which we've a perfect right to do by the way, seeing they've been coat-trailing through our streets all their lives. The time for us to stay in our ghettos is gone. The rednecks will react, they'll be violent and the RUC will side with them. There'll be Fenian blood spilled but it's the only way the world's going to see what sort of a place this is."

"But what if that brings out violence on our side?" I asked and was right away sorry I'd spoken because I'd given her another opening to ridicule me.

"Well then you've got the revolution getting moving haven't you. That's how politics works you see."

These words were said slowly, so slowly, as if I was an idiot or something. I wasn't about to take that sort of ridicule from anybody, least of all this bloody fly in the ointment.

"So it's orange versus green is it? You're hoping to dig the IRA up out of their graves? How does this fit with all the socialist stuff you're on about? All these intersections?" Good that, I thought.

I saw the anger building across from me and heard Aisling start to say something and then stopping.

"There are two things you have to understand,"

hissed the dyke, nostrils widening. "Number one, I *am* talking about a socialist revolution here. And number two, to get the thing started you have to bring matters to the boil and then you lance the boil you see, bring out the badness."

"She's right Jeremiah," Aisling said reasonably. "If this doesn't come to a head soon it'll go on generation after generation. It has to be dealt with. The other things can come later. All-Ireland socialist republic, integrated comprehensive education, nationalisation of the banks, cancellation of the Third World's debts."

Jesus. I stared at her. "Do you really think, Aisling ..."

She waited. Patient, raising her hand to quieten Frances who looked ready to let fly again. "What? Do I really think what?"

I lowered my eyes. "I don't know," I said. "It all seems so, I don't know, inconsistent."

"In case you didn't realise," said Frances, "no worthwhile political change has ever been brought about without violence. Do you think the people of Poland are going to get their rights by sitting on their backsides?"

"For Poles read Fenians?" I asked. Her face flashed with hate. I smiled bitterly at her sitting there themed in black like one of these freaks you'd see in the front of the National Enquirer or something. Was Aisling out of her mind or what going to bed with that?

"The word you should be using is imaginative, not inconsistent," said that. "But if you prefer to live in some kind of armchair dreamland, well...all I can say is, your political ignorance is staggering." And she turned her head away from me and shook it at the wall.

Aisling spoke, her voice a little shaky. "The march on the first is based on the Selma marches in Alabama. Sixty-five wasn't it Frances?"

"March sixty-five. Selma to Montgomery. There were some broken heads there all right. Bloody Sunday the first one was on. The police laid into six hundred of them with their billy clubs. Sunday the seventh of March it was."

"There's one thing I'm not looking forward to," Aisling said, "and that's John Hume and these ones trying to hog the limelight when we get back to Derry on the fourth."

"How do you mean?" I asked.

"Well, unless there's a blue moon those four days we're going to get a rough ride all the way from Belfast. And the minute we land here you'll have these middle of the roaders that haven't an original political idea between them standing up spouting from the backs of lorries with the TV cameras on them and most of us will probably be in casualty."

"Sure it's the same all over the place, sure what do you expect?" said Frances. She seemed to weary then, the effort of going on talking not worth it anymore. She gripped the arms of her chair and raised her ugly bulk slowly to a standing position, then straightaway plodded to the toilet without another word. We heard the bolt noisily secured and looked at each other.

"Stay, won't you," she said softly pleading.

"How?"

She looked around her helplessly. "I wish you and Frances had got on."

"How? How can I stay?"

"Do you want to?" I wished we were alone so I could have her right then. Maybe right there standing up when Frances went to bed. Or. I looked at the sofa next to me.

"I love you," I said. "I wanted to see you, I tried to find you I don't know how many times. I wanted to tell you I was all right about Audrey. I'm sorry for what I said that night you came to the wake."

She covered her face with her hands and sobbed into them. I sat there trying to get the right thing ready to say for when she was able to listen again. She took away her hands then and her eyes and nose were running. The toilet flushed noisily and Frances emerged heading straight for the bedroom looking at nobody. "Night," she said.

"Goodnight Frances," Aisling said. "I won't be long." She produced a tissue out of somewhere. The bedroom door clicked closed.

"Audrey showed me things." Shoes clattered dropped deliberately. "I tried to tell you. She brought me out of myself ways I never thought could happen." She wrestled at her nose with the tissue, then folded it carefully in four and slipped it up her sleeve. "But I would nearly have left her that time for you even though it would have broken my heart."

"What time?" I stood up. Now can I hold her? We're alone now.

"The last night I saw you. Not counting Armagh. The night of the wake. Maybe if I'd met you before I met her I'd never have taken up with her. But then ..."

"Then?"

"Then I couldn't have loved you the way I did. It would just have been like it was with the others before you, the same old thing over again. I never loved in my life before I met her, do you know that, Jeremiah? I'm talking about everything, *every*thing, I'm talking about trying to accept people being different, Protestants, blacks, Indians, Muslims, Jews, anybody coming to live here."

"Was that it? Tolerance? Was that what she taught you?"

"And that God's in everything. Also that God's in everything."

"But I thought you didn't believe. You said it yourself. That thing you just said there was one of the first things we learned in the catechism."

"You're not listening, you're not letting me finish. It's churches I don't believe in. She was twenty-two and it was as if she was here before, honest to God. Did you ever hear of Spinoza? Or Karl Krause?"

"I don't think so." This was doing my head in. Why couldn't we just get down to it? And talk later.

"It's so simple when somebody explains it to you. God's in everything, He's in nature, He's got nothing to do with priests and churches, right? Who wrote the Bible? Men, the whole sixty-six books of it. You wanted to hear her, Jeremiah. Eve was made up and the apple was made up and the whole world swallowed it. For thousands of years women have been living inside the boundaries made for them by men. Like, who says women can't love each other? Men. And men say it's a heresy to think God could be in nature. You know why they say that? Because it would only lose them their power. If God's in nature then they've no control over Him because nature's a law unto itself so that means men can't be go-betweens anymore, they can't interpret and twist. Where would they be then, the ones in Rome and Canterbury and Jerusalem and all? If people can find God outside in the fields or with their lovers where does that leave these people in their marble halls?"

"They lose their dominion I suppose."

Her eyes filled with brightness. "That's exactly the word Audrey used. Dominion. The second time I was ever speaking to her she said to me, I won't allow any church or state to have dominion over my body. How dare they! That's what she said. How dare they!"

"Could we turn off the superser?"

"What?"

"The superser. Could we turn it off? My head's spinning with it."

She got up quickly from her chair and switched it off. "I'm sorry. I wasn't thinking." She was closer to me now, standing not four feet away. She blinked. Can I hold her now I wonder, I thought. "I'll have to get an electric heater," she said absently. "I'm always intending."

"It's just the fumes," I told her. "Probably I'm spoiled. We've got a coal fire you see."

She nodded. "You know why it struck a chord for me? What Audrey said? My father. My father did what he wanted with me for two years nearly and then with my little sister and these people think ... these people are just as repulsive as he was. Who do they think they are anyway?"

"God's gift?"

She gave a little yelp of approval and quickly crossed the space between us. Then standing very close to me she put her arms around my neck. I could only think of one thing. I gripped her and held her hard against me, so hard she gasped. When I found I was hurting her I loosened my grip a little and our mouths kissed. I'm not sure how long we stood that way, bodies together, lips soft and warm. Near the end of it I slid my hands from her waist and fingered the leather skirt. She didn't resist at first but soon drew back from me.

"Take it easy, that's sore," she said but her eyes were smiling. "Why don't you come in with us?"

"What?"

"Come in with us. Frances will be fine with it."

"You don't mean ..."

Aggressively she tongued my mouth, then slid her hand behind the buckle of my belt and turning away pulled me after her like a trolley. "Come on. Honestly, it'll be all right."

It was more than all right: reader, it was wonderful. Frances grumbled at the start and threatened to go and sleep on the sofa but after some coaxing and cuddling from Aisling which I manfully tried to turn a blind eye to she accepted the arrangement on the understanding that Aisling lay between us.

It didn't take me long to appreciate the advantages in this unique situation, being turned on greatly extra by making love right next to Frances kept wide awake and knocked nearly out of the bed three times at the very least on account of our exertions. I'm not going to try and tell you that I got permanently even after all the outrageous slings and arrows I'd taken from her but for those heavenly minutes at least it was as if they'd never happened and she looked like a beaten docket by the time Aisling and I settled.

But then possibly the best part of the night, next to unbelievable in fact. As I lay pretty much out for the count on my stomach bathed in a molten afterglow I felt this rush of icy air and seemed to dream that the bedclothes had been whipped off me. Before I could grasp the what the why and the wherefore I felt a fierce stinging pain on my backside repeated over and over and half turned to see the bold Frances standing on the bed swinging Kitty Birch for all she was worth and roaring out of her like a madwoman. She was stark naked now and a very different animal from the academic I'd briefly got to know and hate.

My sideways glimpse angled upwards revealed a woman with rictus leer and invisible eyes like some grotesque Greek statue come to life. Then for no reason I could understand at that particular time the pain eased giving way to titillating tingles, what amounted to a second wind in fact, the urge to start again in other words, and I heard Aisling whimpering beside me. I must confess that with all the turmoil happening I'd temporarily forgotten her. My mind to be honest was on Kitty who I realised had been withdrawn from my person though I knew from the vicious swish of her that she was still about and I ached to be flayed by her again. But quickly I began to understand that Aisling was the one presently getting it so I lay still, mind racing, waiting, hoping the beating would turn her on before I faded.

The strangest things happened then, outside and inside of my head in slow succession: fumblings, fondlings, footerings and the thought that maybe you didn't have to like someone to enjoy their company in bed, the growing understanding that as long as you worked with your eyes closed you could loathe them yet not be loath to doing the business. Anyway, what with one thing and another I ended up between the two of them, Frances and Aisling, and between the two of them it ended up I could hardly lift my head. But somewhere in the middle of everything I had this notion that the bedroom wall was coming in and it took a while to grasp that it was only our next door neighbour above Mickey MacTamm's barbers trying to make contact.

"Trollop! Bastard! Christ I don't know which of the two of yous is worse. I'm phoning the police if yous don't stop it right now, you hear?"

I actually thought he said priest and this put me in a bit of a temporary state brought on I have to admit by the Catholic rule of thumb which teaches that if ever you come across heaven on earth then as surely as night follows day hell will soon be coming up on the inside behind it and consequently during that minute or whatever it was I was picturing the parochial house across the road flooded with light at three in the morning give or take, and Bishop Farren and Father Hourigan and a whole collection of them summoned from neighbouring parishes shuffling over to Aisling's flat in solemn procession with bell book and candle to pronounce excommunication.

+++++

Frances's father is a crooked property owner and she says she's going to shop him come the revolution. But for now she's biding her time living rent free in one of the plush houses he has up the Malone Road that's only a short taxi ride from her studies in Queen's University. Plush isn't the word when I come to think of it, the place is obscene.

Obscene is probably just about right actually because a lot of the time during every weekend which I now spend up there I should tell you, there are happenings in the pink active sexfriendly ultra king-sized airbed (twelve by ten) that I can hardly bring myself to write freely about even in these decaying months of this most decadent of decades. If the truth be told it's like Sodom and Gomorrah there sometimes. And what was the other place? Edom, if I remember right from the Teachers' Guide to the On Our Way catechism. Edom where they did things arseways. A la mode. When in Edom as they say.

I'm telling you this not as a voyeur—even though I have to admit I've done a bit of that too—but as a full-blown participant. Body and soul have no bounds there, reader, need is what drives us up the enchanted slopes, ecstasy is what we get at the top and the good vibrations only stop when we're asleep and not always then either.

You may wonder how I can bring myself to go on lying with Frances given she's got baps like hot water bottles and an arse on her that would put a fully loaded beer lorry to shame and given also she still contraries me every time I open my mouth to speak. But the mind is a funny thing and up the Malone Road it's all smoke and mirrors from the first joint of the day to watching ourselves in action when evening begins to fall. As the poet

Robbie Burns put it after he saw a louse crawling into the lady's bonnet in church: O wad some Pow'r the giftie gie us to see oursels as others see us. A true philosopher if ever I read one.

And then there's also the fact that her bed is a non-aggression zone, an erstwhile no-man's land that I've been given access to. And we tolerate each other there because Aisling is the prize. Plus Frances has this big soft thick rope with all these strands hanging down that she calls her cat of many tales that inflicts maximum pleasure without leaving welts. Also when I'm taking time out I can get quite delirious watching illegal lesbian acts being performed right in front of me like I was King Herod or somebody. For make no mistake about it, even with all the things I feel about Frances and the awfulness of her Adam's apple there's something about one girl surrendering to another that always does the trick.

+++++

Sometimes I asked myself if it was worth it. And then I remembered Aisling and knew that it was. I'm thinking here about the People's Democracy march. Hungover from what are you having in Frances's lust nest on New Year's Eve night I lined up at nine the next morning outside Belfast City Hall next to Aisling and Frances and I don't know how many others. We got a bit of a noisy send-off from a pantomime-looking character called Major Ronald Bunting who's supposed to be a friend of Paisley's. He had a Union Jack and a bunch of men with him and they were singing The Sash my Father Wore in I counted about twenty different keys. This wasn't good for my head or my bowels for that matter which weren't in great shape either from the drinking and being bound up the night before and I'd this terrible certainty they were never going to work again.

    The first day is still a bit of a haze to tell you the truth. I remember the fresh air and the walking easing the headache once we got out past Glengormley but these things are relative. I was still feeling mostly like shit warmed up and the way the police cosied up to the Unionists blocking our way every few miles didn't help. Each time a handful of them appeared somewhere the cops diverted us down back roads miles out of our way and then it took ages to get back to near enough the place we'd been stopped. And we were supposed to be a legal march, it was the other crowd who were breaking the law, blocking the queen's highway. To tell you the truth the only thing that kept me going was Aisling beside me. She's got a way of holding my hand sometimes that's like a promise and this covers a multitude.

The head definitely improved as we came near Antrim and even though I had to listen to taunts like *One Fenian No Vote* and *Tell the Pope to give you a Pill* and some of the cops shouting abuse as well it was all starting to pass me by like the proverbial idle wind. Though Antrim itself wasn't exactly a bag of fun with crowds of loyal Ulstermen I suppose you could call them heaving away at us trying to push us into a river. But it was mostly no bother to me because I'd got Aisling to stay well back and to the side—I thought it was the least she could do seeing I'd come on the march with her—so we were never exactly in harm's way.

We stayed in some friendly hall the first night, don't ask me where. I hardly slept because we had to lie on the floor and use our coats as pillows. I wouldn't have minded too much if I'd got holding Aisling but Frances parked her big arse between us and I didn't feel up to trekking round it in the dark. What made things all the more sickening was just before dawn I heard this moaning and grunting coming from some place over to my left and there was no mistaking what it meant. Life can be one bastard.

The second day it was we picked up the man from Toome. That's what me and Aisling still call him. The man from Toome. We call him that but we don't really know if he was from Toome. All we know is, he joined the march there and he smelled like a haystack and nobody knew him. And he was one of those people you couldn't tell what colour he was. Usually you can tell. Most Protestants have Protestant eyes and a way of talking that gives them away but with this guy you didn't know if he was a real supporter or a Trojan horse because he had eyes that were hard to pin down and he never spoke to anybody, not that I heard anyway.

The thing was, nobody realised he had a

small bag of pepper in his pocket. Well, nobody realised till he emptied it in some Royal Ulster Constabulary men's eyes the next day when they were trying to block our way outside Dungiven.

What happened was, when the cop in charge was telling Michael Farrell—he's the leader of People's Democracy—that they'd got reports of a large angry crowd at the next fork in the road that were planning to attack us meaning we'd have to take a four mile detour along muddy country lanes to avoid them somebody got a passing driver to check it out and he came back and said all was there was a collie dog and two wee girls playing skipping. Farrell told this to the cops but they just stood there stony-faced as if he hadn't spoken. So somebody organised us to link arms and the idea was to walk forward through the police cordon without using violence, just exercise our right to march legally and if something was in our way well we'd just walk through it.

But then the oddest thing. When the RUC and us were glaring each other down a car pulled up and it was Pearse being driven to the airport. He got out when he saw me and came over. He was looking not too bad for someone who was supposed to be on his way to an early grave, that was the word from Big Bill Braddock anyway. "Hey Jerry boy, what in under God are you doing here with this crowd of wankers?"

I wasn't sure what to say because some of the wankers definitely heard him. Ignoring my non-reply he went on: "There's only one way to sort out this bloody circus of a so-called province and that's the gun, boy, the old bomb and the bullet. These people only understand one thing and that's brute force."

"You think so?" I said this quite loudly trying to hit the right sort of reasoning tone with Aisling listening linked onto one arm and Eamonn McCann listening too I'd say, linked onto the other. I half looked round and McCann's jaw was jutting. What the fuck's going on here? it was saying.

"How's Eamonn?" said Pearse throwing a big smile that I think was supposed to disarm but which wasn't returned. He leaned to my ear then and whispered: "Look at history would you. Tell me one case—"

"Right Jeremiah, ready?"

This was a calculated interruption by McCann but it was going to take more than that.

"There's never been a case—"

"It's all right for you saying that," I told him over my shoulder, starting to be pulled forward. "You'll be in Manchester watching Georgie Best and them and we'll be the ones caught up in it here."

"Wouldn't pay to look near them. Hey, I must go. You know I got a reference from Father McGaughey out of the Long Tower?"

"Did you right enough?" There was a thin blue line of smoke rising straight up in the air from behind the cop that was pressed against me nearly like it was coming out of his helmet. Chimney probably. Or something burning in a field.

"I did." He was shouting now. "That bastard Hourigan wouldn't give me one seeing I only gave him two weeks' notice so I went to Father McGaughey. Remember I worked in the Long Tower primary awhile when I came out?"

"Ah, right." It was downright indecent the way me and this cop were pressed together. Like the Embassy ballroom on a Saturday night.

"Get rid of him for Christ sake," whispered Aisling pulling me against the cop so hard his helmet fell off and got caught between his chest and mine.

"Well, McGaughey had no hesitation. Sound man so he is. Makes you realise they're not all bad. Listen, I'll be in touch."

And that was him away. Anyway the cops ended up in the ditch most of them. Michael Farrell was explaining in a loud voice all through the push o war for the benefit of the TV cameras that we weren't using violence, we were just exercising the legitimate right of legal marchers to walk on the road. The trouble was that some of the cops were being blinded by the man from Toome and I heard when I got to Derry that an RUC spokesman made a meal of it when he was interviewed on TV. So to this day I don't know if the man from Toome was trying to help us or blacken us.

But I'm getting ahead of myself. I was going to tell you about the second day. It was on the second day that my bowels moved in a field behind the Ponderosa on the Glenshane Pass and my form lifted. Except my feet were killing me, blisters and calluses and corns, the whole lot, I'll never learn about what kind of shoes to wear. Still, all I could think of coming out of the field was lying beside Aisling again and that bitch wasn't going to get in the way this time.

The Ponderosa is a pub at the top of the Glenshane Pass about a thousand feet up. There's a plaque on the wall inside it saying it's the highest pub in Ireland and this massive boy with a broad Belfast accent that was drinking with Eamonn McCann was arguing away really loud saying he was in one down in Cork that was higher. Or maybe it was Kerry, can't remember. They've a lot to argue about I said to Aisling and Frances and Frances squeaked People need a break but her tone of voice meant Give me a break.

We slept in a hall in a place called Gulladuff that night and I still didn't get near Aisling because Frances got two fierce looking feminists to come over and sit with us and they stayed of course and then when we finally got bedding down the way everybody lay made anything impossible.

In the middle of the night I struggled between all these sleeping bodies to go outside for a pee and when I was shivering doing it this man appeared out of the dark and scared the life out of me and when he was at it he had a good look to see what I was up to, suspiciously good I thought, and then walked on past saying You're all right there, carry on. I could nearly have sworn he had some sort of a rifle half over his shoulder but maybe it was a stick. Anyway he put the wind up me that much I was nearly doing a shit as well.

When I went back in I could see a bit better with being out in the dark and I found my way to our place no bother. I looked to see if I could squeeze in beside Aisling but her and your woman Frances were that close together you couldn't tell where one ended and the other started, so I kicked Frances sort of accidentally twice, one of the times I got her on the head but she didn't budge. I couldn't think of what else to do to express myself and then when I found my place it took me ages of course to get back to sleep.

I was kind of groggy the next day and the only thing kept me going was that we were getting closer to Derry and Aisling's flat and I managed to put the thought that Frances would be there too out of my mind. We all went to the upstairs part of a pub in Claudy that night and I was slurring my words even before I got half way through the third pint. The whole lot of us had to leave together in case anybody got lost and somebody led us across the street and down this long alleyway to a big hall. I remember saying to myself holding Aisling's hand that if I got to Derry alive I was never going to lie on a wooden floor again. Back, feet, neck, the whole lot of me was feeling it and all I wanted to do was go to sleep. I didn't think I'd even be fit to make love in the unlikely event Frances would allow it.

But I wasn't getting sleeping for a while yet. There was a big stage at the back of the hall and before you knew it some self-appointed leaders were up on it, not Michael Farrell because he really was the leader, but these self-appointed ones that started spouting all this stuff about what they were going to do the next day when we got to Derry. I couldn't make much sense of half of it but they weren't going to let John Hume or anybody else from the Citizens' Action Committee steal their thunder, that was for sure.

This guy Mickey Mulcahy that I know, fully paid-up leftwing loophead he is, seemed to be the main spokesman for these ones and it was obvious he fancied himself as some kind of orator. *I have a dream that this country of ours will rise up.* Christ. Martin Luther Mulcahy. It's the firewater, I was thinking, that and probably joints half the day as well. He was calling John Hume and them traitors and collaborators looking for their place in the sun and what was the other thing he said they were doing, yes, that they were out to line their pockets with the queen's shilling when it was our blood was going to be spilt.

Bloody ridiculous, I thought, people with drink in them shouldn't be allowed to just stand up there and influence people like that. I got to my feet really mad and was going to let Mickey know a thing or two but before I could open my mouth somebody else started. "I speak for the silent majority," he shouted, "and I'm telling you now, it doesn't matter who gets the credit. This is about ordinary people's civil rights, not about Mickey Mulcahy feeling miffed." I felt somebody pulling at my elbow then and Aisling all urgent whispered,

"Leave it Jeremiah. Here, sit down," and I lost my balance and fell half on top of her. "You spoke well," she said sort of smiling and she had her hand on my leg, "but you were talking shite." I didn't mind what I'd been talking. I was beside her and she was handling me. She'd squeezed me in between her and Frances and your woman was sitting there with a face on her but there wasn't a thing she could do about it.

The speeches stopped a wee while after that and somebody put the lights out and then, heaven. Last day of the march coming up and it didn't matter if the world ended sometime in the middle of it, nothing mattered except the night and the girl beside me. We didn't speak, we didn't need to, everything she did showed she was mine.

+++++

We were well fed in the morning, big doorsteps of brown bread and butter and bits of bacon on them. Somebody came round too with pots of tea and we drank in turn, I think there were about twenty cups to go round the whole lot of us but it was great. I'd been living on fish and chips mostly for three days so bacon was like caviar, not that I've got the least notion what caviar tastes like. Aisling looked brilliant in her duffel coat and dirty jeans as we started down the road past Desmond's factory and I kissed her again, and then again and again until she pulled back embarrassed.

"Cool it Jeremiah, they'll be throwing us off the march." Her face was so beautiful under the urchin hair I could have eaten it. But there was a problem and that was my feet. I'm talking about a big problem here. My heart wanted to walk with her forever but my feet were wrecked. She knew it too the way I was walking.

"You'll never be able to make it to Derry," she said. "Maybe you should try and get something for it. There's bound to be a chemist's open in Claudy. What time is it?"

"Twenty past ten. I saw one up the street there a bit but if I went back now I'd never catch up with the march."

"Of course you would. Sure I'll go with you. I'll treat your feet and then we can thumb a lift and we'll be back with the march in no time."

Her eyes were burning blue in the morning light. Her gaze was open and loving and she was thinking only of me. I'd say if some genie had made us the offer of being together anywhere else in the world just then she'd have come with me no matter about her politics.

"Right," she said. "Frances, Jeremiah and me are going to get some ointment and dressings. I'd say we'll probably only be about twenty minutes. We'll catch up."

The dyke wasn't pleased. "I don't think you should do that," she muttered.

"Frances is right," I said. "Yous go on. I'll be with yous shortly." I spoke in a mind made up way that wasn't taking no for an answer. This was because the dust and sweat of three days marching was layered on top of a certain amount of ingrained dirt between my toes and I wasn't going to have Aisling seeing and smelling that, not to mention touching it. It was all very well for Shakespeare to say love is not love that alters when it alteration finds but he never saw my feet.

Aisling looked up at me and I thought for a second she was going to cry. "Go now then," she whispered. "The sooner you get it done the better. We don't know what's up the road."

"Just in case I miss you," I said, "how about we arrange to meet in Derry?"

She nodded. "Where?"

"City Hotel. What, four o'clock?"

She nodded again and then she unbuttoned her duffel coat and held me against her in a full-length arms around my neck embrace that wasn't far off making love over again and it was as if she had me up in the air and I couldn't feel my feet. It went on for the time it took the marchers to pass us and they whooped and clapped as they passed. *One man One girl* and *You shall Overcome* and *Aye Ye Boy Ye* they were shouting and hands were ruffling my hair. Then she was away and everybody with her.

I hobbled up the street to the first chemist's I saw and got what I needed. The girl behind the counter seemed to know I was a marcher and when she saw the way I was walking she offered to treat me herself. Good-looking girl too but I had my pride. About fifty yards down the road I found a place to sit, a low wall beside a trickling stream, and I went about fixing myself the best way I could. Then I got to my feet again and started to walk. It was agony. Whatever I'd done I'd made it worse. After a minute or two I found a hen-toed way of going that was just about bearable. But it's funny how your feet can be nearly killing you and you can still take in certain things, like sunlit dapples I saw on garden grass under a holly tree. It was the most amazing midwinter I ever remember, more like the middle of spring. Usually the snow was on the ground at the start of the year but I'd never seen anything like this, a mild sun warming me on the fourth of January. I made my way to the bottom of the street hen-toeing along like the lame boy in the Pied Piper of Hamelin. The lame boy left behind while Michael Farrell led the wonderstruck Marxists into the mountain never to be seen again.

    A car drew up alongside of me and I heard the voice asking "Are you one of the marchers?" Frisson of fear. What do I say?

    "I'm okay thanks." That should do. Walk on. Look straight ahead. I walked on and looked straight ahead. He came after me, easing up to the footpath, first time in my life I'd been kerbcrawled.

"Here, hop in." Legs wobbly below the knees and a rush of something all the way down inside. I looked behind me. I couldn't see anyone, not a soul in sight, it was as if Claudy had emptied. Christ.

"I see you're limping. You were in the march, weren't you? With Aisling O'Connor? Hop in and we'll catch up with them in no time."

"How do you know Aisling O'Connor?"

"Aisling? I met her in the Grandstand Bar in Derry one time before the fifth of October march. There were representatives from about half a dozen political organisations there I think but she sort of stood out. Fiery girl. I'm in the Civil Rights Association." He reached his hand across towards the open window. "My name's Frank Gogarty."

I looked at him properly for the first time. Clean-cut, friendly, gentlemanly. He was trying to help me. I shook his hand.

"Thanks, I will take a lift if you don't mind." I opened the door and got in. "Sorry for being so suspicious. It's just that, you know ..."

"Don't apologise. You're right to be careful.

Having trouble with the feet?"

"It's my own fault. I didn't come prepared. I'm Jeremiah Coffey by the way."

The car eased off. "Pleased to meet you. I don't think any of us did. Come prepared. How could you in this country?

The seat felt so good I could have slept on it. The radio was playing soft music volume low. Something from Brahms maybe, I love Brahms, didn't get a chance to listen right with him talking though.

"I drove down from Belfast this morning just to keep an eye on what's happening. I think these students are amazing. Are you a student?"

"Naw, that's all behind me. I came because I ..."

Why did I come? Not for civil rights anyway. For Aisling. The whole lot of the rest of them could go to hell.

"I think we all come at this from different directions. One of the spurs or I should say two of the spurs for me were Conn and Patricia McCluskey."

"Right?" I'd never heard of them.

"Yeah, they started the Campaign for Social

Justice you remember. They're an example to us all so they are. Never give up, that's their motto. And always thinking outside themselves."

I was nodding knowingly, not wanting to let on.

"How did you know I knew Aisling O'Connor?"

"I saw you with her when I was getting petrol in Claudy." There was a smile in his voice. He'd waited for me to come out of the chemist's and sat watching me probably when I was trying to fix my feet. Why had he done this? I was nothing to him.

"There they are," he said. "They've made good progress."

We eased up behind them and some people at the tail end turned their heads to us. One of them waved. Left hand side of the road, orderly march, solid citizens, you wouldn't have thought some of them were out to bring down the state.

"I could let you out now but if you wouldn't mind I'd like to go on ahead a bit to see something. I'm nervous to tell you the truth about what might be up the road and I want to check it out. I'll come back then and drop you. Is that okay?"

"Okay." A lazy lassitude had settled on me, delayed reaction probably to my night with Aisling and the backlog of lost sleep, and I was so comfortable I felt like I might have to be winkled out of the seat when the time came.

We overtook the marchers then with some toots of the horn and inside of about five minutes I saw something that got me sitting up straight. Just across the road from the bridge at Burntollet there was a line of RUC jeeps and a couple of men with big sticks in their hands were standing talking to four or five cops.

"What about that," Frank Gogarty whispered, driving on trying not to make it obvious he was looking at them but they couldn't have missed his head turning. We went on up the hill at normal speed and when we got round the next bend he did a quick reversing job into a lane and headed slowly back down towards Burntollet.

"We'd better let the marchers know," I said and it was Aisling I was thinking of.

"Hold on, they won't be here for another while yet." And he stopped near the top of the hill, pulling into the left where we could see the men talking to the cops. The thing was, if we could see them then they could see us.

"They can see us," I said. "Maybe we'd better go."

"Take your time. Here, I'm going to get out of the car now to look at the engine. You come with me."

He leaned forward and pulled a lever somewhere and the bonnet gave a nervous jump. The cops and the guys holding the sticks were only about a hundred yards away. Was he mad? We got out of the car and he lifted the bonnet, fixed it carefully on its stand and peered down at the engine.

"Looks all right," I said standing there on my nerves.

"Looks anything but all right. Turn your head round a bit past me. Two o'clock. See up behind where the jeeps are? Can you see? Two o'clock. Can you see the people up there?"

I gave a quick look. The ones I saw were more like matchstick men, hurrying back and forward carrying things. I didn't know what they were until this big jagged-looking stone, more like a middle-sized rock it was, dropped out of one of their arms.

"Christ, that's ammunition. That could kill somebody. And the police know I'll bet you. They must know. We have to stop the march."

"Right, we'll go now. No point in delaying." He dropped the bonnet with a crash and I nearly wet myself. We got back into the car. I sat waiting, wondering why Frank wasn't starting the engine. Then I understood why. One of the jeeps was crawling up the hill towards us. Time seemed to slow to the speed of the thing.

The music was still playing. Brahms' Lullaby, unmistakable. Must be a tape. The jeep took a breather, then changed down a gear. Funny the things come into your head. I was sitting there quaking waiting for the front of the march to come over the brow of the hill behind where the cops were and at the same time I was embarrassed for Frank because I could hear the frightened wheeze in his chest but then when I held my breath to check for certain I realised it was coming from me.

"The marchers will be here any minute," I said.

"It'll be all right. They couldn't possibly

make it in that time. We have to wait anyway to see what our friend wants."

The jeep juddered to a stop right in front of us and a cop got out in stages, deliberately maybe, maybe he was trying to put the shits up us, one leg, then the big bottlegreen ass, then the other leg, gun in holster swaying, baton tucked handy. I couldn't see right but I think there was someone in the passenger seat.

Frank touched my arm. "Say nothing."

"Having a spot of bother there?" I didn't see the face, didn't look at it to tell you the truth.

"No, we're fine," said Frank. "We were just about to head back to Claudy."

"Oh?"

"Yes, I left something behind there, at the petrol station."

"What would that be then? What did you leave in Claudy?"

"My gloves."

"Gloves?" Pause. "Would that not be them there now?"

"Sorry?"

"On the dashboard. Them look like gloves

to me."

In case we couldn't see them he reached his hand in the window and touched a pair of leather gloves sitting in front of Frank's face.

"Ah, those are my spare ones."

"Hm. Very good. And what was it in the engine was bothering you?"

"What?"

"You were looking at the engine there."

"Ah, it was okay actually. I heard a knocking sound and I thought I'd better see."

That would have been my heart.

"But everything seems to be in order."

"It's as well to be sure about these things sir. Licence?"

"Pardon?"

"Licence please. May I see your licence?"

Two men in civvies walked down past the car and one of them called out "All right Bob?" The other one had some kind of a rod under his arm. I saw it better as they walked on. It was a fucking poker.

"Hi lads, take it easy. Thank you sir. Let's have a looky now." He perused the licence for what seemed like about two minutes and then peered at Frank's face. "You're something in this so-called civil rights thing, aren't you, Mister Gogarty?"

"That's right. I'm vice-chairman."

"And the Wolfe Tone thing, society is it they call it? You're in that too?"

"I am. Good Protestant Irishman."

"Well now, are you a Protestant? I wouldn't have thought that now."

"No, I mean Wolfe Tone was a good Protestant Irishman." Smiling. Trying to smile.

"I'll let that pass sir. And who would your friend be?"

"Ah, this is Jeremiah Coffey."

"I'd like your friend to speak for himself if you don't mind please. Name?"

"Jeremiah Coffey."

"ID?"

I already had my licence out nearly sticking to my hand and leaned over to give it to him. Another minute or maybe two, eyes darting back and forward between me and the licence. Then

"Carry on."

We were away. As we drove down the hill towards the clutch of people standing opposite the bridge I could see that the number of civilians had grown. Ten, fifteen maybe, chatting, some among themselves, others to policemen. Frank gathered speed after he passed them, saying nothing. The plum-soft Sperrins lay ranged to our right, undulating and peaceful like on a picture postcard. Normally they'd be coated white this time of year but now they were more like a purple haze.

"They must be close," he said. They were close all right, round another bend, struggling up a hill, two tired banners fluttering. Frank stopped the car and got out, spoke to Michael Farrell and someone else, seemed to remonstrate with them and after a minute came back.

"They're going ahead," he said as he got into the car. He started up the engine, waved to the marchers as he passed them and stopped a couple of hundred yards down the road pulling over to the side just beyond a wide laneway. As he reversed he said, "I can understand why. Some things have to be done. People have to know what sort of a society we're living in."

We chugged in low gear behind the march and when we got to the top of the hill above Burntollet I said, "Can we lock the doors?"

He didn't answer and I felt foolish. No, not foolish, I felt like a heel. Aisling was out there and I'd want to be able to open the door quickly and pull her in. One of those rocks thrown down from the field could kill her. So could a police baton or a beating by one of these boys that looked as if they were going to be let run riot. I was in the middle of whispering a Hail Mary into myself when it all started to happen. Everything was calm one second and the next it was like we'd arrived in the middle of it. Marchers were being hit with sticks and there were stones flying across in front of the windscreen from our right. A girl was on the ground in front of us out for the count and this bullnecked man was still laying into her with something that looked like the leg of a chair.

Where was Aisling? If I'd got out I'd have been no help, they'd have beaten me to a pulp. You could see them coming in legions now carrying cudgels, these weren't sticks, these were big heavy clubs, past the cops standing there with their batons hanging out of their hands. And then the next shock. I was jolted forward and suddenly we were stopped, blocked, we couldn't move, we'd nowhere to go. Wherever she was she wasn't there. I saw marchers scrambling over the ditch into the field to our left and the Prods going after them. Some of them had grabbed ones and were holding them up by the hair the way Indians in cowboy pictures hold up paleface scalps. A boy standing, fifteen, sixteen, different looking from the others, neatly dressed, an ashplant in his hand like you'd have seen an old man with, not sure what to do, standing at the ditch wondering whether to follow maybe, then struck out at the shins of someone running past him.

"That's my banner!"

"What?"

"That's my banner!" Frank was reaching for the door handle. Christ. There he was right in front of us, the major himself, Major Ronald Bunting, the guy that led the singing of The Sash outside Belfast city hall on the first, there he was dragging his feet back and forward as if he was wiping the mud off them on top of a banner lying tangled on the road, then jumping up and down laughing and dancing like a madman. He looked like he was singing too part of the time but I couldn't hear with the doors and windows closed. I didn't see Frank going but suddenly there was a rush of shouting in my ears and the car door slammed and the shouting stopped and he was gone. Next thing I saw him through the silent screen in front of me pushing Bunting away and then I couldn't see right, people were blocking my view and somebody was lying on the bonnet and I was rocking from side to side. Then my door flew open and I thought, I'm for it now, they're going to drag me out.

"Here are the keys. Take the wheel." It was Frank and his face was covered in blood. He was rubbing at his eyes with one hand and giving me car keys with the other. They were slippery. I took them, jerked myself out and let him in. The odd thought occurred to me, I think it was then or maybe it was later, hard to know, that I wasn't covered to drive someone else's car, in other words once I sat behind the wheel I'd actually be breaking the law and in front of I don't know how many policemen too.

How I got round the front to the driver's side through the milling attackers and marchers was weird. I don't remember it all but I remember the cop and the club. I bumped into the back of a cop and said sorry. Sorry. I told him I was sorry. He didn't move, he didn't turn, and I had to go round him. There was a club with two nails in it on the road next to his feet and I picked it up. I think maybe I was thinking this might puncture our tyres but it could have been some instinct was working there somewhere, like nobody was going to go for me with that in my hand, none of the marchers anyway and none of the attackers, definitely not. So for whatever number of seconds it took me to get through the mill and the mayhem I was near enough untouchable. And the funny thing is, to this day I couldn't tell you what I did with the club. I know I didn't take it into the car with me but I don't remember dropping it.

"I'm sorry to put you through this." He'd got a towel out of somewhere and had it on his head. "Could you drive me to the hospital?"

"Okay. Sure." The cop was in the way. The keys were sticky and slimy at the same time and I dropped them twice before I managed to switch on the engine, found the horn and sounded it. The cop turned round. I smiled apologetically for giving him a start. He looked at me frowning. I smiled again, eyes open wide, eyebrows raised artlessly, trustingly. Let us through please, I smiled, we're innocent travellers, we've just come on this unfortunate whatever it is and we need to get through. If you would be so good. Somebody outside my window screamed "Please! Please don't! No! No!" I raised my right hand respectfully to the cop, gave the suggestion of a wave and hoped my demeanour was right. Respect above all else, respect was what was needed here. He turned and began to walk slowly backwards, waving us towards him like he was on point duty, looking to right and left, saying some things to men with clubs. I moved forward in first, car jumping as I struggled to get used to the clutch. Don't let it cut out, I cried to myself.

"My God, look at that poor girl."

I mechanically followed Frank's gazing direction and saw a heavyset woman that looked like Mussolini in drag being beaten with fists and her nose spurting. It was Frances. I looked around for Aisling but she wasn't there. The cop was staring quizzically at me, beckoning away at me, and I found I wasn't moving. I raised my hand smiling cringing and drove slowly on.

"Here, stop. Help her into the car."

"I can't. If I try and do that we're finished. They'll get me and that won't help any of us."

He didn't answer, saw the sense in what I was saying I suppose or maybe decided he was in the hands of a heartless bastard. Suddenly like fog lifting the road was clear in front of us and the cop was no more and I put the boot down and before I knew it we were in Drumahoe. Sleepy Drumahoe with watchers standing sentinel on footpaths waiting. Then Altnagelvin Hospital, trying to remember where the turn to casualty was. I could have cried I was that relieved.

"You'll be sorted in here I hope. How do you feel?"

"I'm all right. I'll be all right. It'll take a lot more than sticks and stones."

"I'll wait for you. Just need to find a parking place here."

"No, I'll tell you what. Just leave me off at

casualty and drive on into the city. I'm not going to impose on you any further, I've put you through enough."

Looking for the turn to casualty. "But what about you? How will you?"

"I'll find my way to Guildhall Square. That's where they're going to assemble. I know Derry. Could we arrange to meet a certain time somewhere and you could tell me then where you've parked the car?"

"Okay. Let's see, what time is it now? Right, how about half three in the City Hotel? You could be ages here waiting."

"That's the job. Just drop me here. Is this the entrance to casualty?"

"Aye. But I don't like leaving you. It doesn't seem right."

"I'm safe now Jeremiah. I'm not going to bleed to death." Smiling war-painted face under the red turban. "Thanks, you've been brilliant."

I drove into Derry, past crowds gathered at Irish Street like for a carnival on a newly-mown grass banking littered with mounds of stones, into a city with traffic starting and stopping in ordinary ways. Brilliant. Is that what I've been, is that what I am, the brilliant self-preserver? Well that's okay isn't it, that's the human impulse.

I found a parking spot near the top of Bridge Street, walked away looking back at number plate, feet crucified, keys sticky-dry in trousers pocket. Tyrone registration, should be safe, mixed bag of religions up there, bag of cats. What a bloody country. Kings and tribes at each other's throats long before Westminster, before the Normans, before Christ for Christ sake, the most distressful country that ever yet was seen.

What did you call the guy that brought the Normans here over some woman he was banging? Dermot MacMurrough, that was him. Bring me the head of Dermot MacMurrough. And his balls too when you're at it. And out at Burntollet protesting Protestants programmed to attack any threat to their way of life and more of them at Irish Street also stating their Britishness. Give me love, give me you know what any day and everything else can go to hell. Where is Aisling? If she gets by Burntollet she'll only have one more gauntlet left to run. I'm worrying about her now I'm safe, worried about myself when I was scared. But sure that's the way anybody would feel. She'll be fine, she knows how to take care of herself. Run Jeremiah, run, she said in Duke Street the day of the fifth and she ran too. I was batoned and none of them touched her.

A girl coiffured to the eyeballs bumped into me turning the corner at the bottom of Bridge Street fumbling in her handbag for something. Nice smell off her. Sorry she said and smiled. Not a patch on Aisling. Protestant eyes too. She'll be okay. As long as she didn't see Frances getting punched and go and try and help her. She wasn't anywhere to be seen, they were well separated, she wouldn't have got involved. I'll see her in the City Hotel at four o'clock if not before. How long's that? Plenty time.

Foyle Street was bad and getting worse the further I got on it. I thought of septicemia. Maybe I should wash the two of them, wash them and treat them, might even take a bath and all, get the whole hog cleaned. Be set for tonight then. Nuisance, time-consuming, but still be worth it. Taxi! Thanks, thought you weren't going to stop there. Marlborough Terrace please. Christ, what did I say? Dead giveaway. Fenian written all over it. I appreciate you stopping, good to get sitting down. My feet. No, no, I wasn't marching. It's these corns, let them go too far. That's right, Marlborough Terrace. Yeah, I heard that myself. Somebody said there was trouble out past Drumahoe somewhere. Terrible country.

+++++

I kept my two dates at the City Hotel. Aisling was waiting outside for me and I kissed her so long and held her so tight people were looking.

"Oh thank God. You smell lovely Jeremiah. Are you all right?"

Red mouth to her red mouth, washed against her unwashed and the smell of last night still off her.

I took a breath. "I'm fine. What about you? I was so worried."

"You know me. Survivor. I'll tell you later. Will we go inside for a bite to eat? Unless you want to stay and listen to the speeches?"

Some girl speaking through a sound system

outside the Guildhall was calling Derry the capital city of injustice. Clever that. Bit of an exaggeration but still, speechmaker's licence.

"Naw, we'll go in, is that okay? I'm starved with the hunger."

Inside I found Frank Gogarty and gave him his keys. He had a neat professional bandage on him like a white skullcap and was looking not bad considering, feeling reasonable. I did the introductions but they remembered each other anyway. From the Grandstand. Smiling pleasantries, car's in Bridge Street, do you want me to show you, not at all, I'll find it, pleasantries again, thanks, handshakes, goodbyes. People that pass in the night.

"That's a really nice man," said Aisling.

"Amazing man. You wanted to see the courage of him. He actually owns the civil rights banner that was carried on the march you know."

"Owned. I saw it being burned."

"Aw dear. Tell us, how long has Frances to stay in?"

"Two days at least. She's lucky when I think of it. If I hadn't seen her and dragged her away it might have been too late you know."

"Will we ask for a menu? That food smells lovely whatever it is."

+++++

We heard trouble as we lay together that night. Sometime before we went to sleep it died away. In the morning we listened to the Radio Éireann news about the police invading the Bogside in the middle of the night singing *Hey hey we're the Monkees* and beating people up. A man came on saying he rang the police to tell them the RUC were in the street outside kicking in doors and breaking windows and could they send someone.

But all this was months ago. There's another kind of chassis now because the prime minister Captain Terence O'Neill had to resign for being too moderate and another branch of the aristocracy has taken over don't you know, chap I hardly heard of before called James Dawson Chichester-Clark. Aisling reckons he's going to go at it with both barrels. The place will be like Dawson City, she says, before this cowboy's finished. She showed me an interview Terence O'Neill gave the Belfast Telegraph after he resigned. I can nearly rhyme it off it's that good. *It's frightfully hard to explain to Protestants that if you give Roman Catholics a good job and a good house they will live like Protestants because they will see neighbours with cars and television sets. They will refuse to have eighteen children on National Assistance. If you treat Roman Catholics with due consideration and kindness they will live like Protestants in spite of the authoritative nature of their Church.*

Ah, our Church. He got that right anyway. The authority of the Church that has us bending the knee handed down by boys like Augustine who for the best years of his life got up on everything that moved and rumour had it some things that didn't and then turned to God for something that would do him for when he was past it. Father of the Church now, biggest slagger off of women ever born after having spent half his life shagging them shitless, declared marriage a necessary evil, evil because it involved a dirty three letter word ending in X, necessary because how else were the numbers in the Church going to get any bigger? God's ways are not our ways and all that, but what can you do? And who's this else there was? Of course, their royal highnesses Solomon and David, who when they weren't writing psalms and stuff for the Bible were having it off with whatever took their fancy. Lecturing to the chosen people and lechering with whomsoever they chose.

And now that I'm on a roll there's Paul the Sixth in his marble halls in the Vatican popetificating to women that are dying in childbirth and of course our bishop Doctor Farren in his palace across the street from Mickey MacTamm's barbers with its twenty-five rooms, the palace I'm talking about here, Mickey only has the one if you don't count the toilet, honouring us with his presence on Corpus Christi and Easter Sunday and the like as he lords it down the middle aisle soaking all and sundry with holy water. And the priests. Hourigan. Swindells. Cullinan. Finucane. My God, how many bad apples does it take to make a barrel rotten? Or is it the barrel that makes the apples bad?

And yet. And yet they have me in their thrall still, they seduce me with their sights and sounds and smells, to this day I'm a sucker for their incense and their rituals and their Gregorian chants, they frighten me half to death with their pictures of hell.

The truth is, reader, I've been hearing about hell since I was knee high to a grasshopper and I can't get it out of my head, that place Our Lady showed little Lucia and the other Fatima children in a vision with its burning blackened demons that used to be people walking about like you and me.

But then I say to myself, how can this be, who told us about this? Lucia, that's who, ten years old, poor indoctrinated child, hearing about hell since she was knee high to a grasshopper, imagination going like wildfire, grew up and became a nun and wrote her memoirs that faithfully told of hell again but now in more measured language. It's like my brain breaks free for a while and tells me the Church is giving me crap but my soul is triggered to shrivel up at certain times when they go on about eternal punishment and it's always for sins of the flesh I can't help noticing and not financial corruption like you might get in the Vatican bank for example. They've had me twenty-eight years now and it doesn't look like they're letting go easy.

But I started to turn the corner a bit round about the middle of February there, Valentine's Day in fact. Talk about appropriate. This Spanish priest

Father Morales, or Father Juan Francisco Morales to give him his full name, came to the cathedral on some sort of exchange scheme and he was a godsend, a man sent from God whose name was Juan.

I only went to him in confession because I was stuck seeing Father Finucane was away taking his place in Barcelona. Anyway, the first time I went I told him about sleeping with Aisling, holding my breath like to see how he'd take it, testing the holy water as it were. It turned out he'd the most amazing attitude, so much so I nearly peed my trousers with joy right there in the confession box. You love her? he asked. Yes, oh yes Father, but she won't marry me, she doesn't believe in marriage, she says it's manmade. Then stay with her, he said, and convert her if you can. Pray, pray for her and you will see, God will reward you. But is it all right to go on making love to her, Father? Oh yes, absolutely, this is very important. Always remember that love is the greatest of all things, like the rainbow that God sent after the flood it overarches all other things.

This man could be mad, I thought, but he could also be exactly what I want. He's a priest isn't he? He's my confessor isn't he? So then the next time I went I told him about the bondage, breaking it to him in stages if you follow me, and later the three in the bed thing, *but that's only two days out of every seven, Father, and I have to do it to hold onto her.* I couldn't see him right in the dark of the confession box but I'd a feeling he wasn't batting an eye.

The fact that he went away with John Pius Allbright at the end of May, to Las Vegas I heard though nobody has ever actually confirmed that, I heard other people saying the Canaries, in no way affects what he told me. If what he said was true for those three and a half months then it's still true. Just because he turned out to have certain tendencies doesn't make what he said invalid, right? He didn't deceive anybody, he never pretended to be heterosexual, not like John Pius did. Married and all too, death on homos Michael Cole was telling me, queer sort of a queer hater he said, never out of the parochial house, lived in the priests' pockets, prize prick in other words. Allbright he fell, proud carrier of the canopy over His Lordship Bishop Neil Farren's head up and down the middle aisle every Corpus Christi and Easter Sunday and so on and so on. Shows you, doesn't it? I still don't know what Father Juan saw in him but there you go.

The other side of the house lapped it up of course but plenty of our own crowd as well. He's Juan too, some of the vulgar ones said, takes Juan to know Juan, cheap shots like that, but I'll bet you anything even the holiest of the holiest on our side had a good sniff of satisfaction to themselves when they were going over their rosary beads. It's the *News of the World* gene in everybody, that's what it is, this craving for the gossip. Next to love it's what makes life worth living I suppose.

When I think back, John Pius Allbright was a pillar of the church from ever I remember. Actually when I was about ten I used to think he owned the cathedral gates, the ones at the bottom of Creggan Hill I'm talking about. You'd see him there every Sunday in his three piece suit with his big buck teeth like Horatius at the bridge stopping drivers getting into the cathedral grounds if they didn't have a pass.

I remember the time I got a car first I applied for a pass because Mammy was acting up about her legs and said she couldn't walk the two hundred yards to the cathedral but no, John Pius wouldn't give me one, said there were a limited number of parking places in the grounds and our case wasn't deserving enough but I could park round by Great James' Street and bring Mammy in through the sacristy if I wanted. I didn't really care because that way was just as handy but she said Maud told her John Pius only gave passes to his friends so I challenged him one day, on principle you understand, and he's blanked me ever since. I'm not even sorry for his wife because she's a prick too. At least there's no children. But you want to see the cathedral grounds now since he's gone. Things have gone to pot, who gets parking seems to be down to natural selection, the survival of the thickest you could say.

+++++

I got a letter from Pearse last week.

```
Jesus Christ you wouldn't believe it man,
you can breathe here. Do you see that town
over there, that town was suffocating me.
You should get out, I'm telling you. I've
got a job till July in a nondenominational
```

school and it's great. The children are barking but it's great. I'm busted half the time paying a fortune for this rat trap of a flat I'm in but it's great. Derry gave me the pip, I reckon it was Derry put me on the drink in the first place listening to people that had the backbone of a fruit fly not to mention the culture of a cockroach. And that's not even talking about the Father O'Flynns that have brought the place to its knees. The whole bloody country's down with rabies if you ask me with their medieval religions and politics, emphasis there on the eval.

Tell us this, did you ever wonder how in hell Ireland turned out so many great writers? Well that's it. I've just said it, they turned them out. On their ear. Bloody well chased them. I don't think there's another place in the world celebrates mediocrity the way Ireland does.

Anyway I'm on the wagon again, back with AA and all. I'm going to whack it this time. You know what else is wrong with the ones in old Oireland Jerry? They're hooked on the colonial yoke, that's what, it's the serf thing, minds frozen in aspic. I'm not counting you and the other dreamers I saw taking on the cops that day I was leaving, absolutely not, you and them are deemed extremists by the high and wise, but sure you know that anyway don't you?

Even the ones over the border in the so-called Republic of Oireland that are supposed to be shot of the Brits can't get enough of the queen and of course their excuse for a parliament in Dublin is nothing but old wine in new bottles, did you ever hear them talking? The rubbish?

And you know what it is? Their minds were that long in jail they're like a man when he's let out after whatever number of years gets all jittery and goes and starts rattling at the prison gate to be let back in.

Or you know what it's like? It's like those sad cases that would do anything nearly to get the shite beaten out of them by some dominatrix. God knows who our fellow countrymen would get to abuse them if the miracle ever happened and they got browned off with Queen Lizzie and Holy Mother Church.

You'll have to excuse the rant Jerry boy but it's only when you get out of that place that you really begin to see it for what it is and then the anger wells up. By the way I take it you escaped the attentions of the Stormont delegates at scenic Burntollet? Somehow I couldn't see you letting yourself get a second dose after the fifth of October in Duke Street. More important, are you getting ass? Because nobody deserves it more than you. What about that mad Marxist that got you batoned? She's probably the only thing that'll save you from Rome. Then hand in your notice and get her to come to Manchester with you. No security of employment here as far as I can see but sure security is the enemy of progress.

    Take it easy,
    Pearse

No address. How does he expect me to write back?

+++++

So we're living here in sin next to Mickey MacTamm's shacked up in the shadow of Saint Eugene's. And the clergy are on to me, I can see it in their eyes how their eyes avoid mine. At the time of writing they haven't made a move but I suppose they'd be within their rights to sack me for giving scandal, Catholic teacher in Saint Ignatius's primary dragging their name in the mud and so on. Maybe when the bishop holds his next monthly meeting of the parish priests of the diocese over there in the parochial house and they're shooting the crap about this and that, maybe then the subject of Jeremiah Coffey will come up.

    Even if they decide to keep me on rather than airing Ignatius Loyola's smear-ridden linen in public I know I'm never going to get promotion but I've got Aisling which is more than all the heads and deputy heads in the world put together could ever even fantasise about in a million years. Or the priests and bishops in their finery and fancy cars. Or the pope and his cardinals with their vassals and serfs running round tending them hand and foot.

And Mammy? Mammy will just have to lump it. I know she's down on her knees half the day and night and she's never out of the cathedral lighting candles to Saint Monica that her son will do an Augustine. No chance of that, not for now anyway Lord. Maybe if I get a sickener, pick up some kind of infection from Frances, I'll turn out to be Augustine Mark 2 but somehow I doubt it. She should be grateful actually, Mammy that is, she's got Majella McAllister staying with her now. Remember her? The Majella that French-kissed me at Maud's wake? The same girl would have stayed for nothing because she's been lusting after me since we were about nine and she'd do anything for me. I'm talking literally here.

"Five pound a week all right Majella?" I asked her.

"That's too much Jeremiah. You're far too generous." Her big brown heifer's eyes were eating me up the two minutes I was standing at her door making the offer. Invited me in and all but the last time I was in there she pulled my trousers down and I ran home crying. So I wasn't going to take the chance. She's a very strong girl, muscles on her like, who do you call her, Boudicca, be all right maybe if you were desperate.

"When could you start?"

"Anytime you want Jeremiah. I'm on my own now since Daddy died and I'll be glad of the company. I'd start tonight if you wanted."

I'll say she would. She knows the score about me and Aisling but her attitude is she's prepared to wait. In the meantime she's keeping my bed warm. Mammy put her in the back room but she only stayed there the first night because the bed was too lumpy she said. So now she's in my room. It occurred to me as soon as I walked away from her door actually that she looked like one of those ones that would be right and thorough with the cleaning and dusting and all and it wouldn't take her long to ferret out the black plastic bags with God knows how many pairs of dreamspattered underpants and three pyjama bottoms if not more in them. And the Woolworth's bag behind the bath. And I don't think I ever got rid of the pair of corduroy trousers I ruined with that girl from Bishop Street. Wherever they are, too late now. The whole thing's sort of embarrassing but no doubt she'll put them to good use.

So for now anyway, routine. Aisling won't get married but we do everything a married couple does near enough—except for the Malone Road and the cat of many tales that is, both of which look as if they're going to go on awhile yet—plus I've turned into a bit of a community activist, out there trying to get the rioters to go home, real do-gooder, scared I'm going to get my head in my hand some day if I look at them sideways though.

And then there's the other kind of fear which is far worse. Juan Antonio's spirit is still there but it struggles sometimes and I'm asking myself how much longer I can go on believing there's no such thing as that kind of mortal sin as long as it's done for love. The fear comes out of the dark when I waken up in the middle of the night certain times and think, What if I died before the morning, where would I go, does every penny of this not have to be paid back? And then I touch the brown scapular I've been wearing since the Carmelites gave the retreat in May and I feel better. Aisling's okay about it, amazingly okay actually, but she says I shouldn't wear it in bed, it would serve me right if I got strangled making love with it on. And where would you be then? she says.

I wish I had her certainty about hell not being there. How is it people are so different? I can hardly stand the sight of some of the priests now but I still need their rites and their penances. I take the partial indulgence granted by Pope Benedict the fifteenth to those who devoutly kiss the scapular with a pinch of salt but I believe the virgin Mary's promise to Saint Simon that whosoever dies wearing it shall not suffer eternal fire and also her revelation to Pope John the twenty-second that all who wear it will be released from purgatory on the first Saturday after death. And then sometimes I'm thinking, wise up, there are no Saturdays in purgatory (only Mondays Aisling says), these things should have gone out with Santa Claus, you're a grown man for Christ sake.

But old fears die hard and this is going to take me awhile. In the meantime I say to myself that life without Aisling would be a worse hell than anything the devil could serve up. And if there's such a thing as heaven on earth then this is it. Happy daze.

ALSO AVAILABLE FROM NUASCÉALTA TEORANTA
www.nuascealta.com

Three Leaves of a Bitter Shamrock
Jonathan Swift, Liam O´Flaherty
and Tomás Mac Síomóin

Three wildly imaginative essays, written in three different centuries, propose grotesque and outrageous solutions to the social problems created by the established political order, especially unemployment and austerity.

The House of Gold
Liam O'Flaherty

A rare perspective on the Irish at a major turning point in their history. Greed, priestly lusts, sexual frustration, alcoholism, and murder are themes woven together in this compelling tale.

GiB - A Modest Exposure
Jack Mitchell

An epic poem attacking the system that cloaked the murder of IRA members Daniel McCann, Sean Savage, and Mairéad Farrell by British security forces in Gibraltar.

Printed in Great Britain
by Amazon.co.uk, Ltd.,
Marston Gate.